In the center the stood with perfect pos... **dark suit, looking like… She could not articulate it, but she suddenly understood the novels she loved to read.**

He was perfectly polished, looked every inch the prince in his bespoke suit and crisp edges, but something in his eyes felt...wild. Which was ridiculous and likely her imagination.

She moved closer, meeting his gaze and feeling... something she could not quite articulate. She had not expected...whatever this was. Because it went beyond nerves—she knew exactly what nervousness and being out of place felt like. This was bigger, deeper. Less about her and the world around her and more about something...internal.

Perhaps it was simply that he looked *at* her. Not with the hate her father did, or the complicated push and pull of worry and disappointment her mother did.

No, he looked at her as if she were a riddle to be solved. Maybe it was just new. She'd been stuck in the same old place, being the same old person for so long. Maybe this was a fresh start.

Marrying a stranger.

Rebel Princesses

Two princesses forced into a lifetime of hiding...
Two men to show them who they really are!

Zia and Beaugonia, twin princesses and heirs to the Kingdom of Lille, have only ever had each other. Growing up in the shadow of their crowns and royal expectations, Zia has always been there to protect Beau—against the world, against their powerful parents... But now she's disappeared!

When Zia discovers that a rare night of freedom has left her with a life-altering consequence, her only choice is to flee the royal spotlight. But she can't hide for long from the man sent after her—Cristhian Sterling, finder extraordinaire...and the father of her twin heirs!

Read all about it in
His Hidden Royal Heirs

With her sister missing, Beau must step up and take her place...by standing in as the bride at Zia's royal wedding! Could the man meant for her sister be the one to finally set her free?

Find out in
Princess Bride Swap

Both available now!

PRINCESS BRIDE SWAP

LORRAINE HALL

PRESENTS

Harlequin®
PRESENTS™

ISBN-13: 978-1-335-93925-8

Princess Bride Swap

Copyright © 2024 by Lorraine Hall

For questions and comments about the quality of this book, please contact us at CustomerService@Harlequin.com.

TM and ® are trademarks of Harlequin Enterprises ULC.

Harlequin Enterprises ULC
22 Adelaide St. West, 41st Floor
Toronto, Ontario M5H 4E3, Canada
www.Harlequin.com

Printed in Lithuania

MIX
Paper | Supporting
responsible forestry
FSC® C021394

Lorraine Hall is a part-time hermit and full-time writer. She was born with an old soul and her head in the clouds, which, it turns out, is the perfect combination to spend her days creating thunderous alpha heroes and the fierce, determined heroines who win their hearts. She lives in a potentially haunted house with her soulmate and rambunctious band of hermits-in-training. When she's not writing romance, she's reading it.

Books by Lorraine Hall

Harlequin Presents

The Prince's Royal Wedding Demand
A Son Hidden from the Sicilian
The Forbidden Princess He Craves
Playing the Sicilian's Game of Revenge
A Diamond for His Defiant Cinderella

Secrets of the Kalyva Crown

Hired for His Royal Revenge
Pregnant at the Palace Altar

The Diamond Club

Italian's Stolen Wife

Rebel Princesses

His Hidden Royal Heirs

Visit the Author Profile page
at Harlequin.com.

For anyone struggling to know their worth.

CHAPTER ONE

PRINCESS BEAUGONIA FREJA CAJA ISABELLA RENDALL sat sandwiched between her parents in the back of a sleek car that was winding through the curving roads of Divio, a small principality nestled in the southern Alps.

Her new home.

She supposed she was nervous, in a way, but she was also filled with purpose. She knew every step forward—no matter how far out of her depth, no matter how challenging—was in aid to her twin sister.

She owed Zia everything up to this point, and now she would return the favor.

She supposed a lifetime married to some crown prince she'd never once met was quite the sword to fall on, but Beaugonia had seen no other choice. Zia was *pregnant*, and in love with the father of her children—whether either of them wanted to admit it or not. Beaugonia may not be an expert on love herself, but she'd certainly read her fair share of books on the topic.

And certainly her sister couldn't be expected to marry the crown prince of Divio in her state, even if Lyon Traverso would have married her already pregnant with another man's twins.

Unlikely.

Which also meant Zia couldn't be expected to continue on her life as heir to Lille.

Beau could have left it at that. Her father was a king and had the power to choose whatever heirs he liked— that was why Zia was heir in the first place, despite the fact Beau was three minutes older. But Beau had never been the ideal princess.

Maybe that, in part, was why she'd concocted this plan. Not only did it take the heat off Zia, but it ruined her father's plans. He couldn't *choose* an heir if she'd set herself up as one he couldn't hide.

Beau had reached out to Lyon herself. Even before Zia had been reunited with the father of her babies. The moment she'd learned of Zia's pregnancy, Beau had begun laying the groundwork, and Zia's upcoming wedding to Cristhian Sterling only pushed her plans into high gear.

Underneath her father's nose, Beau had gotten the agreements *herself.* So when she'd presented her father with her upcoming marriage to the crown prince, her need to be his heir in order to accomplish it, he had not had a choice.

He could embarrass them all and break off her agreement with Lyon, refuse to name her as heir. Or he could accept what she'd done. And she'd known, based on the way her father had treated her for the entirety of her life, he'd never choose embarrassment.

He'd berated her for what she'd accomplished once she'd informed him. If they'd been at home and he'd discovered what she'd done, instead of at Cristhian's estate out of the scope of King Rendall's power in Lille, he likely would have done a lot more than hurl insults at her.

But Beau didn't see the point in worrying over things that *hadn't* happened. She had plenty of worries in the present.

Like marrying a man she'd never met aside from emails and a spare few phone calls.

The car wound its way up to a staid, *ancient*-looking castle, majestic mountains soaring in the distance. The sun was just starting to set behind it, creating the kind of breathtaking scene that might ease the struggle of whatever she'd gotten herself into if she got to look out a window and see that every morning.

Neither parent had said anything on the flight from Cristhian's to Divio, not on this drive from the airport to the castle, and that didn't change as they were helped out of the car and led toward the castle entrance.

But as the doors opened, and they were ushered into a soaring room of archways and stained glass, full of stone and carpets and history you could practically see in the shadowy corners, her father finally spoke.

"We will go along with this farce, Beaugonia," he said in that icy, furious tone he wielded so well. Not loud enough other people might hear, not hot fury that might show to anyone around them. Just pure, cutting ice only she, and her mother, would hear or feel. "But you will not come crying to me when it is a disaster of your own making. If you embarrass me, I will end you."

Beau wanted to laugh. Cry to him? When had she ever? She'd cut out her own eyeballs first.

So she said nothing to him. She just waited as they'd been instructed.

The prince appeared at the curve in the staircase. She had never met Lyon Traverso, but she knew this was him from pictures. An older woman followed behind him. His mother, the countess, Beaugonia believed.

He *was* handsome. Even aside from pictures, Zia had always confirmed that. In the flesh, it seemed less a fact to accept and file away and more an actual…*entity*.

He seemed so *tall* gliding down the staircase in his dark, bespoke suit. His dark hair ruthlessly styled, and every moment as precise as a very sharp blade. The whole *state* of him seemed to back up the oxygen in her lungs. Such a strange response to one man.

Of course, so much about this man determined what her future would be like, so she supposed this feeling of being rooted to the spot was simply…anxiety. That's why it felt like carbonation in her chest.

He approached them, greeting Father and Mother first before he turned to her. His dark eyes took her in, and though she was usually very good at reading people from just a look, she had no idea what the expression on his face meant. Or hid.

And still, this was her fate. A fate she'd concocted for herself. Maybe they wouldn't love each other, but they had an understanding. A mutual agreement that Beau had negotiated herself. Perhaps it wasn't better than love, but it was certainly better than whatever her parents had.

She smiled at Lyon, willing herself to play a part she'd never been any good at playing. *Sweet, accommodating princess.* "It is a pleasure to meet you, Your Royal Highness." She offered her best approximation of a curtsey.

He bowed in return. "And you. Allow me to introduce my mother. Countess Ludovica Traverso." He gestured to the woman still standing behind him. She greeted them all with a regal politeness.

Her expression was easy enough to read. Distrust written into every sideways look.

"The wedding will be held in the chapel at nine," Lyon offered. "My staff is at your service, of course, so you may ready yourself in whatever ways you need."

"I'm still not understanding this *private* royal wedding situation we find ourselves in," the king blustered, as he was likely to bluster until the end of time.

The prince did not so much as even blink. Beau wasn't sure he moved, exactly, but he gave the impression of being very *tall*, as though he were looking down at her father from a great distance.

She very much wanted to learn that trick.

"With the change in brides, we find ourselves in a delicate situation. I thought that was clear?" Lyon posed this as a kind of question.

The kind of question no one dared answer.

Father cleared his throat. Mother looked away. The countess studied Beau's dress as though she were cataloging any wrinkle.

"We will reconvene then. Marco?" He gestured a staff member over.

And that was it. Beau was led away from her one and only meeting with the man she would marry in just a few short hours.

She felt the tickle of panic at the back of her throat but breathed through it. They both knew what they were getting themselves into, and that was all that mattered.

"She's pretty."

Crown Prince Lyon Traverso's mother said this as

if it were some kind of *shock*. He glanced at the countess. "And?"

"You know as well as I do that the Rendalls keep her as far out of the public eye as they can. I expected…" Mother trailed off, likely because she knew whatever she'd been thinking was not appropriate to say, even just between the two of them.

And the truth was, Princess Beaugonia Rendall *was* pretty. Not quite in the way her sister was. Princess Zia had been taller and more…effortlessly regal, it seemed to Lyon. Though he'd thought less of her looks and more about how she'd suited his purposes.

But Beaugonia had made a case that *she* would suit his purposes instead now that Zia was…well, it wasn't clear *what* had happened there, but Lyon had heard rumors.

And as much as he needed heirs, they needed to be legitimate and his own. So a wife who understood that, agreed to that, was far more important than her appearance. As long as she understood her place, everything else was immaterial.

Beaugonia seemed to know her place.

But, he could admit because his mother had brought it up, Beaugonia *was* pretty. Softer, smaller than her sister, and she held herself with a strange…reserve was the only word Lyon could come up with. A reserve that didn't match the cutting quality to her eyes—an intriguing array of shades coming to some sort of hazel conclusion.

In the privacy of his own mind, he could admit that he *was* a bit surprised as his mother had been. Maybe, without fully thinking about it, he'd expected exactly what his mother was getting at. A reason that the princess had been hidden away and Zia had been trotted out as the true royal.

"I do hope you know what you're doing," Mother said, moving about the room, the anxiety all but radiating off of her.

When was it not? Their position was precarious. Because he was not the son of a crown prince, or even the grandson of one.

Which came down the maternal side of things, and the kingdom of Divio had *concerns* about what that would mean for their young leader, shoved into the princehood— the highest royal step here in the principality of Divio— after a series of unfortunate events.

But Lyon was ready. He knew how to be a leader, and he knew his family belonged on the throne, regardless of the whispers. His grandmother had raised him to believe that this would be his fate—because she had known her brothers and their progeny would not last long.

She had always said they'd been train wrecks from day one. Selfish, careless and ruled by wants over any sort of duty.

She had been right. After his cousin's fiasco, there had been a vote to get rid of the monarchy altogether. It had not won, but it had been *close*. Any hint of scandal, and Lyon had no doubt Parliament would hold another one.

So all the training Grandmother had put him through had paid off thus far. He'd spent the past year, almost, trying to earn the trust of his country, with not a whiff of a demand for another vote.

Beau was the next step. A wife. Children—enough that there would be no question, no future concerns of who the next leader would be. Tradition. Respectability. Everything a citizen could want from their royal family.

Not one *whiff* of the scandal the other princes had loved to traffic in.

"She knows what's expected of her," Lyon said to his mother. To assure her. To assure himself. He'd had much longer to determine Zia's appropriateness, but what was one sister compared to the other? Zia had known her role, and so Beaugonia did too. He had spent the past few months ensuring it.

Maybe he hadn't met her in person as he might have liked, but he had made every other effort to ensure her offer was in good faith, and would not come back to haunt him. He had not found even a *hint* of scandal with Beaugonia, the little-known Rendall.

She was perfect. He'd make certain of it.

"We can still put this off, Lyon. Make certain she's the right answer. It took us months to decide Princess Zia was the correct choice. You've switched over to her sister in a matter of days."

Which wasn't true. He'd been exchanging correspondence with Beaugonia for months. But he'd kept that from his mother, and he didn't think it would assuage her fears any to let her know now.

Lyon turned to her and smiled. "I have it all under control. I will not disappoint, Mother."

She studied him, her dark eyes impossible to read. But she smiled in return. "Your grandmother would be very proud of you, Lyon. You were her greatest hope."

Yes. Grandmother had always told him that. He'd tried to carry that weight, but it tended to fit around his throat like a hand…squeezing. So much so that as a teen his mother had taken him to a therapist for his anxiety and he'd been put on medication.

His own failing, he knew, but his grandmother had never known, and he'd kept his anxieties under control thanks to those things ever since.

Lyon desperately wanted to loosen his tie right now, but he knew what his mother would say about that. She would worry even more than she already did that he was not in control of things. Particularly his own anxieties.

So he focused on keeping his breathing easy, his smile relaxed. He would make his mother proud, his grandmother proud—the way no man in her family ever had. It was his sworn duty.

His grandmother's brothers had taken the role of crown prince with more and more disastrous results. Their children hadn't fared much better. Divio had not seen a royal last more than two years in a generation.

Lyon would change that. And Beaugonia would be an essential part of it. She would be acceptable, she would know her place, and she would provide him with heirs, because this is what he'd decided.

And Crown Prince Lyon Traverso always accomplished what he decided.

CHAPTER TWO

BEAUGONIA COULD ONLY stare at herself in the full-length mirror. She looked like an entirely different person in this beautifully elegant white gown. A whole team of people she didn't know had swept in and done her hair and makeup. They had placed a glittering necklace of royal jewels on her neck. Her mother had provided a Rendall tiara.

Beaugonia was used to nice things, being a princess and all, but Zia usually got the full glamour treatment. Beau didn't go to parties or events. She wasn't seated at dinners. Her *faults*, as her father liked to call them, had meant she'd been hidden away for most of her life.

So she felt a bit like she was playing dress-up. Like this was all make-believe.

She wished Zia was here, though Zia didn't know what Beau was doing yet, by design. Zia would try to… stop this, no doubt. But she had Cristhian and the twin babies she was growing to worry about.

Still, it would've been nice to have *someone* on her side with her. Beau felt surrounded by enemies. Which was an exaggeration of course. People had to care about her to be her enemy. None of Lyon's staff thought much of her beyond their job. She was little more than a doll to them.

Her mother watched with shiny eyes and clasped hands like this was all a joy. And Beau wanted that to warm her, but she knew she was only in this strange position because her mother had never stood up for her. Or Zia.

Mother had never been an *active* enemy, but she had always been a passive one.

Father was somewhere, no doubt grousing about how she'd pulled one over on him, but he could hardly ruin anything without making their own kingdom look badly. So while he was an enemy, per usual, he was a neutered one.

That brought Beau some joy. That and the fact that tomorrow they would leave, and she would not really have to deal with them much anymore. She would have her own life. Her own kingdom.

No more locked rooms. No more being hidden away. She would finally be…*someone*.

"You look beautiful," her mother said, with tears in her eyes.

Beaugonia managed a smile at her mother. A woman who meant well but had no backbone. No…fight. She had let her daughters be bullied and threatened and manipulated their entire lives.

Beaugonia loved her mother, but she could not respect her, or lean on her, or trust her.

Beau was alone.

You have been on your own these past few months and you have done very well, she reassured herself.

She even gave her reflection a little nod in the mirror. She might miss Zia, but she was doing all of this for her sister.

And that alone would get her through.

Beau knew better than to worry about panic. A panic attack would come or it wouldn't, but worrying about *if* she would have one would only exacerbate the problem.

Things had come too far to be derailed by the attacks that had gotten her labeled *weak*, *an embarrassment*, *defective* and so on. This was a new life.

She had faith that she could keep her panic attacks hidden from Lyon. Particularly in a castle the size of this one. Divio wasn't known for wanting to hear from a *princess*, what with all their outdated ideas about male heirs and so on. Besides, once they had said heirs, Beau wouldn't need to spend much time with Lyon at all. She could just focus on being a mother.

A future that filled her with hope and joy. Maybe she hadn't thought much of being one before Zia had fallen pregnant, but now she thought... She wanted the chance to be everything her mother had never been. She wanted the chance to love, as fully and unreservedly as she loved her sister.

It wouldn't be her husband, but it could be her children.

"We will move to the chapel, Your Highness."

Beau smiled at the staff person and allowed a whole passel of people to lead her out of the room she'd been getting ready in and through long, wide hallways. Ancient hallways. How many women had walked down these halls in a fancy white dress to marry a man they didn't even know?

Probably quite a few. She wasn't unique. She was taking her place in the rich, bizarre tapestry of royalty. It was kind of like joining a club. And since she'd never been able to join much of anything, this felt like a positive spin on things.

She was brought to a halt in front of giant, dark wooded doors while a staff member whisked Mother off. So Beau was left with only the stern woman who seemed to be running tonight's event.

They waited there for ticking moments while Beau felt her heart beat faster and faster. What were they waiting for? What was she doing?

And just about the time she thought she might blurt out some ridiculous excuse to turn and *run*, the woman stepped forward and pulled open the chapel door. She gestured Beau inside.

And there was nothing to do but step forward, into the chapel.

It was a huge rook. Soaring ceilings, colorful stained glass. Much more ornate than the chapel back home which had a cozy, sturdy quality to it. This felt…delicate. Elegant. She could picture generations of Divio citizens and their pride in such a feat of architecture and art.

She almost smiled. Though she preferred sturdy and cozy, there was something genuinely uplifting about the way humans in all their faults and frailties could somehow put together something that looked like this.

A nudge had her remembering herself. She wasn't meant to stand here and gaze at the stained glass adoringly. She was meant to walk forward. She was meant to marry the prince.

There were few audience members as she walked

down the long aisle, trying to remind herself to be graceful and calm instead of her usual efficient march.

The countess sat on one side in the front pew, her father on the other. A few staff members standing in the shadows, except the one currently ushering Mother to her seat next to Father.

And then in the center there was Lyon. He stood with perfect posture in a dark suit, looking like… She could not articulate it, but she suddenly understood the novels she loved to read about reformed pirates.

He was perfectly polished, looked every inch a prince in his bespoke suit and crisp edges, but something in his eyes felt…wild. Which was ridiculous and likely her imagination. Nothing Zia had ever said and no correspondence she'd had with the prince herself pointed to anything other than a very contained, careful, determined man.

She moved closer, meeting his gaze and feeling… something she could not quite define. She had not expected…whatever this was. Because it went beyond nerves—she knew exactly what nervousness and being out of place felt like. This was bigger, deeper. Less about her and the world around her and more about something…internal.

Perhaps it was simply that he looked *at* her. Not with the hate her father did, or the complicated push and pull of worry and disappointment her mother did. Certainly not with Zia's fervent loyalty and overdone protective instincts.

No, he looked at her as if she were a riddle to be solved. Which wasn't romantic in any way, and she didn't expect romance, she just didn't know why the effect of it all on her was one of...anticipation.

Maybe it was just new. She'd been stuck in the same old place, being the same old person for so long. Maybe this was a fresh start.

Marrying a stranger.

Condemning herself to the unknown.

Saving Zia and her babies.

If nothing else, for the rest of her life, she'd be proud of herself for that. She would stand tall in *that*. Besides, what was trading one jail for another? She'd get to be a mother in this one. She'd get to have some kind of role instead of being hidden away.

So yes. No doubts. No regrets. Only *I do.*

Lyon watched Beaugonia's approach. She looked lovely in white, her dark hair swept back. The dress was a bit much, but she walked under the weight of it with an elegance he had perhaps not expected of the Rendall twin who'd always been hidden.

There was a determination to the set of her shoulders as she approached, but there was something in the way her gaze darted about the large room that gave a slight air of...inner timidity, underneath all that outer strength.

This was good, he assured himself. It would endear her to the public. Confidence was important, grit to a certain extent, but the hint of something softer under all she had to be as crown princess was...intriguing. Would be intriguing, to the citizens she needed to win over.

When she finally reached him after the long walk down the aisle with soft strains of music playing, she expelled a careful breath, then turned to face him.

He'd expected to see nerves on her but was gratified by the grim kind of battle light in her hazel eyes. She knew what this was, and that was all that mattered.

The minister began with his greetings. Lyon only listened with half an ear, studying his bride-to-be. She studied him right back.

It was an odd situation. Even odder than his original arranged marriage. Perhaps because he'd gone out of his way to choose Zia, and he'd had ample time to ensure she, and her family and her kingdom would suit.

The woman before him had searched *him* out. Had left the king out of all their plans. Had been…determined. Even now, her determination to see this through was clear. Quite the turn of events from her sister who had been…wary if reluctantly willing.

Still, the identity of the sister did not matter. He would give Beaugonia all the same things he'd been determined to give Zia. A good life. A strong partnership. Children. Perhaps there would not be love or the freedom to do whatever she pleased, but Lyon was certain stability was better than all of that.

He was given the cue to agree to enter into marriage and offered a solemn "I do." A few words later, and Beaugonia was doing the same.

"You may kiss your bride," the minister intoned.

Her gaze flickered for just a moment at that. There were certainly some aspects of this arrangement that needed to be discussed that he had not felt comfortable putting in the emails and phone calls that had occurred in the past two days solidifying their arrangement.

But a kiss to seal the wedding ceremony was necessary and accepted, and while he and his mother might know this was a business arrangement, while Beaugonia herself might know, he wanted the whole of Divio to buy into the potential for a love story.

In other words, he wanted the photo op. So he dipped his head. He paused for a moment, waiting for her eyes to lose that wide-eyed *trapped* look about them. But they didn't. So he leaned closer, until there was just a breath between their mouths.

"Breathe, *tesoruccia*," he murmured. Low enough only she could hear. "It is only the brush of lips."

Her breath shuddered out, and this…did something to him. He did not know how to characterize it. A strange… *sensation*. Effervescent and light. When for as long as he could remember his life had been about carrying the weight of what needed to be done.

He wasn't sure he liked it, but that same responsibility demanded he not draw this out any longer. So he touched his mouth to hers. And, as he'd promised, it was only the slight brush of lips.

Nothing more.

No matter how it felt like *more*. How it opened up interesting possibilities of what *more* would need to entail eventually.

He straightened, trying to not let the wariness inside of him show on his face. Because there was…*something* there.

Attraction, simple as that, he supposed.

He had not expected any hint of chemistry with whomever his bride turned out to be. That wasn't the point. He wasn't sure he *liked* it, but he supposed as long as it was under his control, it might be useful.

"Welcome to your new kingdom, *mi principessa*," he offered.

She sucked in a deep breath, then nodded. "Thank you, *mio marito*," she returned, with decent enough pronunciation of his native tongue, all in all. She had clearly practiced, which was a nice gesture. One he appreciated.

Because the newly minted Princess Beaugonia Traverso was going to be everything he needed. There were no other options.

CHAPTER THREE

BEAU SAT THROUGH a tasty if uncomfortable post-ceremony dinner. Her father had gotten uncharacteristically drunk in public, and Mother had been forced to pretend he'd fallen ill and get help to usher him away.

His angry gaze had been focused directly on her, and she supposed she would have to count herself lucky that Lyon had wanted this ceremony and dinner to be small and private before they announced their marriage to his people tomorrow morning.

Once the king was out of the room, her entire body relaxed involuntarily. Father was gone. It was unlikely he'd stay around after his behavior this evening. He'd likely be totally gone by sunup.

She was free now. Of the king and everything he'd threatened her with for so long. She wanted to simply sag and cry in relief, but that feeling was tempered by a kernel of worry.

Because the idea of *freedom* begged the question she'd been avoiding. If Lyon knew about her shortcomings, would he have his own threats against her?

Well, it didn't do to dwell on it. The only thing she could think about was having children. *That* seemed to be Lyon's only concern really, and that would protect her.

She hoped. She'd make certain it did. Maybe she had no great examples of what good mothering should look like, but as she'd told Zia only a few days ago, they had an example of what it *shouldn't* look like, so that should be enough.

Besides, Zia was only weeks away from becoming a mother herself. She would learn the ropes and help Beau when it was her turn. They would be partners in this voyage into motherhood, as they'd been in everything else growing up.

Once Zia forgave her for stepping in and marrying Lyon, taking over as heir.

The dinner wrapped up. They were given congratulations by the staff and Lyon's mother. The countess said very little, but Beau didn't miss the way the woman studied her with suspicion.

Then Lyon was leading Beau out of the ballroom, his large hand on the small of her back, while her white skirts swished around. Feeling a bit like shackles at the moment. The idea made her want to laugh out loud, but she swallowed it down.

Up staircases, down hallways. Lyon said nothing, just led her, and she had no choice but to go along. Because he was her *husband* now. Because she thought she knew what she was doing.

More hysterical laughter wanted to break free. Who did she think she was, charging in to rescue Zia? To one-up her father? She should have stayed locked in a room, huddled in a corner. Maybe she belonged in one of those asylums her father always threatened her with.

Eventually, Lyon stopped at a grand door and opened it. He gestured her inside. Into what was clearly *his* suite.

From this grand sitting room, she could see into a bedroom. Everything very elegant and well-appointed. But very...*masculine*. Not a floral or pastel in sight.

She hadn't let herself think too much about this. A wedding night. Maybe she'd been in denial enough to think he'd show her to her own room. With her own bed. With a staff to help her out of this dress. That the idea of *making heirs* might be introduced...later.

Instead, it was just the two of them. They were alone here and she did not know what he expected of her. She stood in the middle of the sitting room in this rather cumbersome wedding gown and wondered just what she thought she'd been doing.

"I realize immediately sharing a room might not be the easiest or most comfortable thing," Lyon offered. He *looked* perfectly at ease. Perfectly...in control. Like he knew exactly what he was doing. While her heart clattered around in her chest, thinking about the way he'd kissed her in the chapel.

Breathe, tesoruccia.

She needed to look up what *tesoruccia* meant.

"Unfortunately, for the optics of everything I'm trying to sell, it's important to act out the facade that we are... more traditionally married," he continued. "It's best if our union seems as genuine as it possibly can be, even inside the castle, so there's no question."

"Even though your country thinks you were engaged to my sister?"

"I was engaged to your sister."

"You had a business arrangement with my father. That is not quite the same. Do they even know that engagement was broken?"

He frowned a bit at that, and she knew she should have kept it to herself, but…well, it was hard not to correct people when they were flat-out wrong. One of her many flaws, she knew. One she'd promised herself to improve on in order to make sure this worked.

"No, but I am quite certain the previous engagement will work in our favor. The story will be that I sought a political marriage, but then I met you and fell in love. We hid the truth from the press until we could make certain…all parties were satisfied."

She supposed that might work. The positive to her mysterious status as the hidden away Rendall was that, really, anyone could believe anything about her. There was no way to prove anything about her was false.

Perhaps *she* might wonder why someone like Lyon— gorgeous and powerful and clearly very self-possessed— might be swept away from his princess fiancée by the likes of *her* lesser princess self, but she supposed that was up to his palace aides to conjure up for the press.

"We do not need to have this conversation while you are uncomfortable," he said, gesturing at her heavy dress. "Your things have been unpacked, plus a few items added for the responsibilities of the next few days. Please consider this space yours as much as mine."

She looked around and tried to imagine treating this space as *hers*. She wasn't sure that was going to be possible, but she also knew getting out of this dress wasn't going to be possible. And there was no staff hovering around to help her. Unless he called someone, and she had a feeling that wasn't in the cards.

For the *optics*.

She cleared her throat. "I cannot undo the buttons on the back of my dress on my own."

He had no facial reaction to that, but he did pause a moment. "Ah." He paused again, then moved forward, gesturing her to follow. "Come."

She followed him into the bedchamber and then into a huge en suite that led to another door, behind which was an entire closet and dressing area nearly as big as the bedroom itself. She peered around the room. She could see one side was clearly his, and one side was…hers.

She thought that this might be the strangest reality check of all time. Her own clothes hung in neat rows directly across from *his clothes*.

"Allow me," Lyon said, holding out his hands.

It took her a few quiet moments to understand he meant that she should turn around so he could unbutton her dress. Which was fine. Maybe the sleeveless nature of the dress meant she wasn't wearing any undergarments up top, but…but…she would just hold the dress up once he unbuttoned it.

She wasn't getting out of it any other way. Besides, whatever this was, she would grin and bear it. That had been the deal she'd made.

Gingerly, she moved so she was closer to him, with her back within his reach. At first, she didn't feel much, just the gentle tug of the dress moving. But as more and more buttons came undone, she began to feel…*him*.

It was such a strange sensation. No matter how often she'd been helped to dress or undress, it had never been a *man* back there. A tall, warm wall of *presence*. One whose fingers occasionally brushed the exposed skin of her back as he moved down the delicate row of buttons.

She held her breath, knowing if she released it some strange sound would come out of her that would no doubt be embarrassing in some way.

"All done," he said, sounding somewhat stiff. But when she turned to face him, his expression was arranged in a bland kind of smile. Even if his dark eyes seemed to...*glint*.

"Thank you," she managed to offer.

He nodded. "You're welcome."

She nearly barked out a laugh. He was her *husband*. This man. She was his wife. Standing in his closet, holding the sagging dress to her chest so it didn't fall. It was all so surreal. She didn't even feel *panic*. How could she? It felt like it couldn't even be real.

"I'll leave you to change." With that, he exited the closet and the en suite bathroom. So that she stood, still grasping her heavy wedding dress, completely at a loss.

What should she change into? Pajamas of some kind? What would be appropriate pajamas for sharing a room with her husband? For *optics*.

Or was he expecting something different? Something more? He'd made very clear the entire purpose of this marriage was for *heirs*. Multiple. Beau might be innocent, but she knew how heirs were made. And she read enough romance novels to know the nuts and bolts of *that*.

She really thought she'd been prepared for this, but the reality of Lyon somehow made it that much more...

She didn't even know how to finish the sentence. That's how little the reality of him matched up to her preparations.

She stared at the clothes in the closet. Some she recognized as hers her staff back at the Lille castle had packed up. Some items were clearly for her, but not her own.

Optics or no, this was going to be their own private bedchamber. She should wear something comfortable to bed. And if he didn't like it…well…

She closed her eyes and breathed out, using all those well-worn techniques to keep panic at bay. Sometimes they worked. Sometimes they didn't. But she was alone, so she wouldn't start adding to the panic by worrying if an attack was coming.

She just counted and breathed until she felt like she was strong enough to make a decision. She'd gone into this knowing she couldn't be herself. She had to be some…made-up version that would suit Lyon. Playing pretend in a way she'd never done before, because it was her turn to take a bullet for Zia.

Zia had protected Beau her entire life. She had stepped in between her and Father whenever she could. Zia had bent over backward to do the things an heir was expected to do, to keep the king from enacting threats against Beau. Beau *knew* Zia was the entire reason Father had never stooped so low as to put her in an asylum. That and how hard it would have been to keep a secret from the press and citizens of his beloved country.

But there was no way to be perfect here right off the bat. She didn't know Lyon well enough. She would have to accept that there was a learning curve and be open and ready for any changes Lyon might want made.

If he didn't like the pajamas she chose, she would march right back in and change. If he told her to do anything differently, she would. And if that started to grate, she would just remember the look of shock on her father's face when she'd told him she'd arranged to take Zia's place in marrying Lyon.

That all the papers were drawn up.

And he would have to announce her as heir.

That memory would keep her going for *decades*.

So, she picked out a pair of comfy leggings from her own clothes and a silk nightshirt. It was hardly lingerie, but there was a kind of sophistication to it that was elegant and could lend itself to anything hands-off...or hands-on.

Filled with determination—or at least she'd fake it till she made it—she returned to the bedroom. To find him unbuttoning his own shirt. His tie was already off, hanging over the back of a chair that sat nestled into a corner by the big window.

He really was beautiful. She knew she hadn't met a lot of men in her life, but he was so tall. His hair had an interesting wave to it, though he kept it short. Underneath the crisp white shirt of his wedding suit, a broad expanse of tan skin, well-muscled and impressive.

Did he work out? He must. No one just *looked* like that, surely, even a handsome prince.

He looked up, and she didn't miss the quick survey of her outfit, though she couldn't read his reaction to it. He straightened, and for a few moments they simply stood in silence regarding each other.

"Now that we have some privacy," he finally began. "We should discuss the more...delicate matters of our relationship."

"You mean sex."

He made a strangled noise. The kind of noise she often brought out in people, but she'd found being forthright and frank often helped quell her anxiety. Just say it. Just deal with the consequences rather than worry about what they might be.

She might have to work on curbing that impulse now, but for this moment, she needed it to keep her steady.

"Yes, I suppose I do," Lyon agreed.

But then he didn't say anything. He stood by the window, shirt unbuttoned. She stood by the en suite door in her pajamas.

He cleared his throat. Which should have seemed like a gesture of *some* kind of nerves, but he stood there looking so…*princely* and handsome and fully in control of himself, she didn't think he'd ever been nervous a day in his life.

"While heirs are my primary concern," he began, like this was a well-planned speech. Maybe it was. "And will need to be…secured sooner rather than later, we do not need to jump into such matters right away. We can get to know each other a bit first. Ease into things."

Beau carefully exhaled. That was actually quite… kind, all in all. She had not thought him cruel—their arrangements had now been a few months in the making. His correspondence had always been polite, his propositions always fair. So it wasn't that kindness *should* be a surprise.

Simply she was not used to it.

He moved then, taking a few steps toward her. Again, her breath backed up in her lungs. There was just *something* about him that drew out these new, overwhelming physical responses in her.

"Just because we have a very careful arrangement

does not mean that it can't be mutually enjoyable. It does not have to be a...chore."

She blinked once. Trying to work through that. *Enjoyable*. She felt her cheeks heat, despite trying to be very *sophisticated* about the whole thing.

"I hear tell that I am not a hideous beast," he said in a soft, humored voice.

It was about the first sense that under all his duty, all his plans, all they'd agreed, that Lyon *might* have a personality. A hint of humor. And ego. Which she didn't mind. She'd much prefer a man who was sure of himself. She'd found men riddled with insecurity who had any kind of power tended to wield it in ugly ways.

"What about me?" she asked him. Because it was true, *he* was gorgeous. *She* might enjoy...things with him. But her...

He gave her a sweeping kind of glance that had a strange fissure of nerves dancing along her skin. "I can see that you are not a hideous beast, *tesoruccia*," he said, his voice...darker, it seemed.

Her body certainly found him convincing, if the heat in her cheeks was anything to go by. But her mind... "You think I'm pretty?"

"Yes."

"Prettier than Zia?"

He raised an eyebrow. "Is it a competition?"

Always. Not because she wanted any competition. Nor did Zia. It was just...how they were seen. Two halves of one whole, but constantly determining which half was better. "No, but that answers the question easy enough."

"Speaking of your sister—"

He wanted answers, and Beau had some, but it felt

wrong to offer them to Lyon. Not before Zia decided on her own fate. "I'd rather not. Not just yet."

He frowned a little, but he didn't press the issue.

"I haven't…" She gestured helplessly at what would be their marital bed. "Obviously. I have been…very sheltered."

"We will take it one step at a time."

"Step?"

"We shared a kiss just this evening. Consider that step one, and enough for our first night as husband and wife." He reached out, took her hand. He rubbed a thumb across her knuckles, then squeezed gently, reassuringly.

His hand was large, warm. It was the strangest sensation, because it sent a wave of nervy excitement through her. That anticipation she so liked to read about.

But there was also a…kindness. One of the few times in her life someone had reached out and offered physical reassurance.

"I think our arrangement will be quite…successful, Beaugonia."

She so wanted that to be true. Needed it. So, she corrected him. "Beau."

"Scusami?"

"My friends call me Beau."

His smile was warm, sweet almost. She knew she shouldn't hope for more out of this arrangement, let all those fictionalized versions of happily-ever-afters give her *ideas*. She was still who she'd always been. A little too direct, plagued by uncontrollable and unpredictable panic attacks, selfish and so on and so forth.

No handsome prince was going to sweep her off her feet.

But maybe…she would hope for a *successful* arranged marriage. Maybe she would allow herself to dream of an arrangement that was kind. And a physical relationship that could be more *enjoyable* than chore.

As long as she kept her true self under wraps, she was certain she could do it.

CHAPTER FOUR

LYON HAD NOT accounted for *wanting* his wife. It was a strange and disconcerting turn of events. He was a careful planner, and while all his life there'd been a certain level of flexibility required of him, he usually considered *every* angle before jumping into something.

It had become apparent, as Beau had walked down the aisle toward him, that he had not considered every angle. Because he'd been struck with the strangest feeling that his world had begun right in that moment.

Which he'd quickly flicked away, a pointless thought no doubt brought upon by the stress of the past few months. First, the knowledge Zia would not be marrying him, and then Beaugonia's alternative plan.

He had been *relieved* to have a plan, a way out of the folly he'd made for himself. It had never once over the months of dealing with Beaugonia occurred to him that Zia's hidden sister might be…interesting. *Or* beautiful.

He had always had to be careful when it came to women. He'd known, even before he'd been crowned prince, that being ruler was the end goal, and there could be no whispers about him that might hurt that eventuality.

He had watched the more wild and reckless members

of his mother's family nearly destroy everything, all for a bit of fun here or there. He'd never understood them.

He had always found it easy to create short, respectable relationships with women, always knowing that he was looking for the perfect princess—above reproach. And when he had not found it, made sure he ended such situations with tact and kindness.

Any errant thoughts about needs, wants, or desires were to be ignored, cut off, shut away.

But now, he wasn't quite certain he understood himself. Or at least his reaction to Beaugonia. Prim and direct at turns. Shy, but not…hiding. The hazel of her eyes was a mysterious blend of colors that seemed to change in the light, with her feelings, or the color she was wearing.

Not that he couldn't *handle* this unexpected reaction, because of course he could. It was just *new*, and thus a little…concerning. He would need to reassess. Go about this entire thing a little differently perhaps.

Because they *would* need to broach the physical requirements of creating an heir, regardless of how he felt about her. He would need to make certain that he was in charge of this unexpected situation of being far more intrigued by her than he wanted to be.

Luckily, she also wasn't *immune* to him. He'd seen the way she'd watched him, particularly when she'd returned to the room when he'd been unbuttoning his stifling shirt and trying to *breathe* past all that…new uncertainty combined with the old anxieties of never quite living up to the expectation held for him.

It was a *positive*, he assured himself as he lay in bed next to her in the dark. Plenty of room between them in his very large bed. Her even breathing filling the room.

He hadn't been lying about his hope that the arrangement would be pleasing. If there was *some* chemistry, the necessities of their arrangement could be enjoyable.

As long as it wasn't *complicated*. As long as it wasn't… he shoved that thought away, but *complicated* lingered, keeping him up all night. He stared at the ceiling, hard and beyond irritated with himself for not being fully prepared for a beautiful, interesting person to now be his lawfully wedded bride.

He needed a new plan. They had hashed out a very clear agreement, but he needed to make certain the realities of their situation didn't undermine said agreement.

He didn't think ground rules were the way to go with her. There was a little spark of something in her—not rebellion, that wouldn't do. Just a very assured sense of self that exuded from her every action, every word.

The woman who had approached him via email a few months ago with news his engagement to Zia would not go through had a very clear determination of how her life would go. It was what had first intrigued him about her offer. The only reason he'd held out on agreeing for so long was because she had refused to meet prior to the wedding.

But she'd systematically and carefully outlined her plan, and he had no choice but to accept the fact that it matched up perfectly with his own. That she offered him more than Zia had, because neither of them would have to pretend.

Except, he had a terrible feeling he was going to have to pretend now, because she was not the icy hermit he'd been expecting.

But he was a married man now. His plan to ensure the

crown stayed stable was moving as it should. His internal thoughts and unexpected feelings wouldn't change that.

He wouldn't allow it.

He would simply get to know his new bride. Engage in that which producing heirs required. And ensure whatever odd sensations plagued him, he was always in control of them rather than the other way around.

As the sun rose, glowing between the gap in the drapes, Lyon carefully slid out of bed and went to the bathroom to shower and try to clear his mind.

It was good, really. To face a challenge that made him sharper and sounder of mind. If things got too easy, he might get complacent and that would never do. His entire rule would no doubt be an exercise in fighting to regain all the control his great-uncles, uncles and cousin had pissed away for the past decades.

Until all that was left was him. Until the entire future of Divio rested on his shoulders. He dressed, though he kept his tie loose for the moment. He told himself he was full of all that determination that had grown shaky after the ceremony.

Until he returned to the bedroom.

She was sitting up in the bed, her cheeks a little flushed from sleep and her dark hair tousled as if he'd had his hands in it last night, just as he'd desired.

She yawned and stretched, looking perfectly...

Well, it wouldn't do to look too hard.

"Good morning," he offered, moving stiffly toward the window. He pulled the curtains back to a bright, snowy day below. He tried to imagine all that *cold* encasing him. "Today I will give you a tour of the castle, answer any questions you have. The announcement and pictures from last night will go out soon, and we'll host a dinner this evening. Then afterward we will film a short video that will go out to news outlets."

"Sounds perfect. I'll just go get ready."

He did not dare look at her even as he heard the rustle of sheets and the soft landing of footfall. He kept his gaze on the window, on the mountains, on all that *ice*.

When she returned, he allowed himself to look at her. She wore slacks with enough swishy fabric not to give much away about the shape of her legs. The dark green sweater she wore was a little more formfitting, but only a little. She looked elegant but cozy. Perfect for the morning ahead.

Because she *was* perfect. "Let us take a little tour on our way down to breakfast," he said, and then began to lead her out of his suite.

It was better in the daylight, he decided. Other things to focus on. *Movement*. Certainly not darkness and listening to her breathe and shift in her sleep. Not hours stretching out in front of him where he couldn't help but think of the way she'd looked when she'd just woken up.

He told her what every door was as they passed. Some he let her peek her head into, some they merely walked by.

"You can of course request to make any changes to our rooms you'd like. It will have to go through Mr. Filini, the head castle master, and myself, but as long as it's reasonable, there should be no problems."

"I doubt very much I'll have any changes."

He didn't know why that settled in him as an annoyance. He shouldn't want a wife who wanted frivolous changes when his entire *goal* was to make certain everyone in Divio looked at him and thought *stability*. Strength. Certainty.

He came to the last door before the staircase and held it open, gesturing her inside.

Her eyes lit up. Admittedly, the reaction he'd been hoping for. She moved forward, reaching out to touch the spines of a row of books. For a moment, she looked around at the shelves and shelves of books—old ones, new ones. Some ancient and passed down from generation to generation, some his own additions.

"It's the most beautiful room I've ever seen," she finally said, breaking the silence. She beamed at him and a warmth of satisfaction settled in his chest.

Perhaps there were some complicated reactions he hadn't anticipated, but a woman who was bowled over by a library was certainly not a bad choice.

"You may of course make any additions you'd like. Your personal assistant will order any book for you."

"But you already have so many."

"No one can have too many books. And no collection should be so rigid so as not to allow entertainment that many users might enjoy."

"My father did not agree," she said, perusing the books. "The books *I* wanted to read, I often had to sneak read digitally through my phone. Which was fine enough, but I always wanted something…" She trailed off, then shrugged, gesturing at the room around them.

Lyon was no fan of King Rendall. The man was a supercilious braggart who used force more than intellect to impose his will on others. Lyon could admit to himself that part of Beau's proposition had been intriguing simply for getting around the king while still uniting Divio with Lille. And he felt that satisfaction again, because a man who imposed limits on reading was no leader.

"Did you always get around your father?"

"Not always," she said, a kind of carefulness about her. She did not meet his gaze. She focused on the books. "But when I could. When Zia and I could. But that makes it sound all bad, and it is not that. He simply cared more about his country than he ever did his children."

Lyon frowned. She did not say it in a censuring way, but he felt slightly…judged all the same. After all, he knew she did not hold her father in high regard, and neither did he.

But Lyon's priority was his kingdom, and he had made that clear. He had to offer his country stability for once, and with that priority came children who would fill their role as heirs. He had never really thought of them as more than that.

But they would be people. Like him. Like Beau.

He didn't like how…complicated that made the future feel. Because the future was simple. They would be the crown prince and princess of Divio and raise children to take their place, and bring Lille into the fold on the death of the current king.

But thought of *heirs* brought him back to the one clear answer he had not gotten from her. The one that left his mother still having trepidation about their arrangement.

Whatever the reason she had not been the heir did not matter. The deal was done. They were married. He would not *let* it matter.

But it was best if he knew before he introduced her to the kingdom of Divio as their princess.

"You're the older twin. You should have been the heir. Is that not correct?"

She shook her head, as though not at all surprised by the change in topic. "That is not how Lille has worked for some time. It was always going to be my father's decision which of his children he wanted as heir. Zia was… better suited. From a young age."

"Why?" He had not asked her this outright, though they had both danced around the subject in their correspondence as they'd worked out the details of their agreement. In the end, Lyon had accepted what she offered was more important than whatever she might be hiding.

He could only hope his instincts had not led him astray.

"When I was very little, before I even fully remember, I found crowds very…scary. I would do all right if I could hide behind Zia, or if I was simply speaking with someone one-on-one, but crowds terrified me. Understandable, I think, but not the best reaction for a princess. Zia, on the other hand, always knew what to say, how to smile and act, even as a toddler. I struggled with this until I was much older. But by that time, I was already defined by my behavior as a child." She didn't look at him as she delivered any of this information. She focused on the books. Then she pulled one off the shelf.

"May I take this one to our room?" she asked, clearly wanting to change the subject.

He shouldn't let her change the topic, as it felt like there were details she was leaving out, but it was still her first day as his wife. He could be kind and patient. "They are your books as much as mine, Beau. You may do what you like."

Her smile was pretty, a little shy. But it dimmed a little when he reached for the book she held. With clear reluctance, she relinquished it to him.

He studied the cover, then flipped it over to the back. "A romance?"

"My favorite. Don't worry. It's not an indictment on my hopes for the future or a romantic nature of myself."

He found himself puzzled, both that she felt the need to preface her statement with *don't worry* and... "Why do you enjoy them then if there's no romantic nature involved?"

She looked at the book in her hand. "As much as I enjoy a good love story, the thing that has always struck me about these types of books is that the main character always finds people who understand them and make them feel...seen. Not just a romantic partner. But friends or family. It's...nice. I like to read about things that make me feel good."

Seen. An interesting way of looking at it, he supposed. He, on the other hand, did not wish to be seen at all. But if she did... Well, he would make a point of it.

"Why don't you pick out a book for me to read. Something that would allow us to have a conversation. A book that would help me get to know you."

She looked at him for a moment as if he'd suggested she take off all her clothes and run through the castle naked. Then she looked around. "I think it will take me a while to decide what book that should be and determine if you have it."

Lyon nodded. "Well, if we do not, we'll have it ordered." He glanced at his watch. "We should make our way to breakfast." He moved to lead her out of the library, but she put her hand on his arm to stop him.

"But wait. What book would I read to understand you?"

He liked it better that she said *understand*, rather than *seen*. Understand he could do. He took a turn about the library. The options were endless. He'd always been a reader, and so many different books had helped shape him into who he was. But he supposed at the center of even his interest in reading was the man he wanted to be. He slid an old tome off a shelf and handed it to her.

She took it, studied the cover, then wrinkled her nose. "A family biography."

"Perhaps a bit dry, I grant you, but that is who I am. Who I hope to be. An extension of the legacy built in these pages. A legacy you are now a part of."

She took a long, careful inhale. "I suppose I hadn't thought of it that way."

"You will be the mother of the future crown prince or princess."

She didn't look up from the book, so he couldn't quite read her expression, but when she finally met his gaze, she smiled. "I think I shall quite like to belong to something."

And he wasn't quite sure why his chest felt...oddly constricted. But he smiled back, and led her to breakfast, ignoring the unknown feeling lurking there.

CHAPTER FIVE

THEY ATE BREAKFAST together and then Lyon gave Beau an extensive tour of the grounds. She kept waiting for him to foist her off on staff. To disappear somewhere, as he had when she'd first arrived last night. But he stayed by her side. She supposed it was so that everyone believed in their marriage as something more than an uncomfortable business arrangement. She could play along.

Happily, she did not feel the least bit panicked though everything was a bit overwhelming. But he had a very calming presence when they were out in the castle. He explained everything. Assuaged every anxiety about settling into a brand-new place without her even having to ask.

When it was time to get ready for the dinner, he introduced her to the team that would help her get ready. By name and position, so she knew exactly who to ask for anything.

The only thing she did not get a say in was the gown she was to wear. When she voiced some concerns about the strapless nature of it, she was assured that everything would be secured quite well.

No one *said* she didn't have a say, but it was clear she was not allowed to *refuse*. She would have been annoyed by that, but she was being poked and prodded and practically sewn into the beautiful dress and she didn't know how to access her anger with all that going on.

She was tired and a little achy and wondering how Zia had done this for years upon years. All this…physical rigmarole to look a certain way for a group of strangers. Events upon events where she had to smile and compliment and act the perfect princess.

All to protect Beau. Because even though Zia had been better at *being* the heir, she hadn't *wanted* it. Two silly, spoiled princesses she supposed, who wanted to be human beings more than some kind of emotionless figurehead.

But Zia had been blackmailed, essentially. Always working to protect Beau from whatever threats their father had leveled at her. And Beau had let Zia take the fall again and again.

Which was why she was here. Taking the final fall. And it wasn't so bad. She'd made her choices, and Lyon was… Well, she couldn't say he was *nothing* like Father, because she knew his kingdom mattered more to him than anything—if she hadn't gathered it from their correspondence, she would have fully understood it when he'd handed her that family biography. Family. Legacy. Tradition.

Yes, she was well versed in how rulers viewed all those things as paramount.

But at least Lyon offered some kindness along the way. Her father had never done that for her or her sister.

The door opened and Lyon stepped in, dressed crisply in a tux, his hair in perfect place. He looked every inch the handsome prince he was meant to be.

One of the women who'd done her makeup helped Beau up out of the chair.

"You look beautiful," Lyon said.

It was a rote compliment, but somehow Lyon delivered it with a note of gravity that made it feel *real*. She had never once felt *beautiful*. Never tried to feel that. She'd always considered it Zia's domain.

Lyon's eyes on her made a compliment she'd never craved suddenly feel…wonderful. And made her think about another night sharing his bedroom. Sharing his *bed*. What *steps* awaited her there.

Which was not at all what she should be thinking about.

"It's as if the tiara was made for her, don't you think, Your Highness?"

Lyon's gaze didn't move from Beau, but he nodded at the hairstylist. "It does indeed."

She didn't *feel* that way at all, but the fact Lyon's gaze stayed on her with such…intensity made her want it to be true. It made her want to stand a little taller and ensure all his compliments could be believed.

It was a very strange feeling, to want to impress someone. From a very young age she'd known that there would never be any impressing her parents, so she'd stopped trying. She hadn't worried overmuch what anyone thought of her because she had known her role. No role at all.

Now she had one.

Lyon took her hand, lifted it to his mouth and brushed a kiss over her knuckles. She wondered if she would ever know how to react to that in a way that didn't make her feel totally off-kilter. Like someone else. Someone who was not unwanted and hidden away.

"The announcement went well and will ensure that we have quite a few attendees at dinner tonight," Lyon said, leading her toward the door. "You will be introduced to some members of parliament. Some members of my extended family. After, we shall sit down and film our short video introducing you and our plans for the future."

"And just what are our plans for the future?"

"A responsible, trustworthy and charitable monarchy that will work with parliament rather than against it and usher Divio into an age of stability they have not seen for decades. A partnership with Lille, that will eventually lead to a union of our countries once you inherit the throne."

She hadn't been consulted in any of that, but then again, she had no actual stake in Divio except for that eventually she would be mother of the heir to the monarchy.

A legacy you are now a part of.

Lyon had said that. Not for an audience, but as if he'd actually meant it. "Will I be expected to speak?"

"My aides have prepared a few remarks for you, yes. After dinner, we will spend some time preparing before we film. It's not live, so you will have ample tries to get it right."

Beau tried not to let that worry her. If someone else had prepared the remarks, she could no doubt deliver them. In fact, that seemed preferable to a dinner meeting people. Having to come up with conversation in a crowd. That seemed far more the kind of recipe for panic.

But she knew the castle now, and she just assured herself if she started to feel the telltale signs—numb feelings in her limbs, tunnel vision, shortness of breath—she would excuse herself and go to the bathroom. Then she would hide.

Worst-case scenario, she'd claim food poisoning.

"You will be introduced to quite a few people this evening, so don't feel bad if you can't keep them all straight. We'll work on making certain you spend time with the people you should know."

"I have an excellent memory for names and faces. It usually only takes one meeting for me to remember people." Her memory had always been excellent. She learned things quite easily, and then they stuck with her whether she wanted them to or not. Her father hadn't cared for her ability to recall things that he'd rather she forgot. Or maybe he hadn't cared for her insistence and inability to let something wrong go.

She was going to have to work on that.

"Quite an asset," Lyon said, patting her arm.

When she glanced up at him, he was smiling. Like he meant it. She felt a strange sweep of...pride move through her. Like earning a compliment from him was exciting.

This was all so...strange. She'd known it would be, but so far it hadn't been strange in the ways she'd been *expecting*.

But Lyon led her downstairs and through a back hallway that would take them to the entrance to the ballroom where they'd be announced. Lyon's mother and a few staff members waited there.

One of them hurried over and said something in low tones to Lyon. Who nodded, but let Beau's arm go.

"I'll be right back." He left her standing there with the countess. Whose expression was…cool, at best.

Her gaze swept over Beau's dress. "You clean up quite nicely, Your Highness."

It didn't really feel like a compliment, considering she'd been "cleaned up" in her wedding dress last night. But Beau smiled all the same. "Thank you. Lyon's staff is superb. I'd certainly be lost if they weren't doing the work to…ah…*clean me up.*"

"I suppose, but could I make one little suggestion?" She leaned forward as if it was some great secret, whatever she wanted to impart.

Beau fought the impulse to lean away. She forced her smile to stay in place. "Of course."

"Perhaps next time you could wear a color more fitting of the royal family," the countess said in little more than a whisper.

Beau looked down at the navy blue. More fitting? She opened her mouth to ask what the countess meant, but Lyon had returned and took her arm and began leading her to the entrance to the ballroom.

Beau looked back at the countess, with the stray thought that perhaps she'd just misunderstood what the countess had said. What she meant.

But the look on the woman's face was clear. It reminded Beau of the evil stepmother in *Cinderella*. Which was so overdramatic she shook her head at herself. There was nothing evil about the countess. Perhaps she'd be a difficult mother-in-law, a judgmental one, but Beau could weather it.

It couldn't be worse than her father.

As long as she doesn't find out.

Beau forced that thought away and focused on the room in front of her. People milled about, then stilled as the announcement came over the sound system.

"May we present Crown Prince Lyon Traverso, and your new crown princess, Beaugonia Traverso?"

Lyon led her forward, when she would have stayed stuck in place. Because while the crowd wasn't *huge*, all eyes had turned toward them. And the countess's comment about her dress color was rattling around in her brain even though it made no sense.

She felt a little tickle at the back of her throat. Anxiety, but not panic. She could handle the anxiety. She'd researched all sorts of ways to deal with the overwhelm of social situations. The panic attacks came out of nowhere. There was little to no warning and often no direct cause.

Lyon took her around the room and introduced her to people. She made certain she looked each person in the eye, smiled and remembered every name and face. Because she could handle that. She was *good* at that.

No matter what color her dress was.

These types of dinners had always felt interminable, but Lyon found himself so fascinated watching Beau that time passed quickly.

She hadn't been lying about a good memory. She seemed to remember everyone by name *and* face. She smiled. She charmed.

Or at least she charmed *him*.

Though he'd known everything would work out with her, or he wouldn't have consented to this marriage. He refused to accept anything but exactly what he wanted, but he felt off-kilter by the fact she seemed…utterly perfect. He'd been expecting a challenge. Hard work. Success, yes, but not without bumps in the road.

He tried to remind himself it was early yet, but the entire dinner went absolutely perfectly. While there were still plenty of parliament members who talked down to him, who did their little political poking, hoping to find a weak spot, he could see on each of their faces they were intrigued by Beau.

He had no doubt the citizens would relish this royal marriage. Some would remain skeptical of his worth for a while longer yet, and understandably so, but once the children started coming, every year he would prove he was here to stay.

They said goodbye to the remaining guests, and Beau said goodbye to everyone by name, impressing each of them, he could tell. Where usually at the end of these types of dinners he felt tired, with a headache drumming at his temples, and his collar all but choking him, tonight he felt...energized.

When his mother came over to them, he beamed at her. "I think we shall count that down as quite the success."

"Don't go counting your chickens just yet," Mother warned, though with a smile. "This is only the very first step."

"But a very good first step. Now, Beau and I must go record our message to the country."

"Beau. How...cute."

But Lyon wasn't paying much attention to his mother. He was focused on the next steps. If the message was well-received, he and Beau would go away for a quick

LORRAINE HALL   55

weekend "honeymoon." At least, that's what the public would consider it.

If not, he would have to have another meeting with his public relations team. Reevaluate and come up with a new plan.

It would be better and easier if tonight went well. Of course, that meant then being completely alone with Beau on a honeymoon. Which was...well, his feelings on it were complicated. Best not to consider it just yet.

"Good night, Mother," Lyon said, giving his mother a kiss on the cheek, then leading Beau away. They would film their message in the library, and then it would be put online and broadcast as soon as his staff got everything edited to perfection.

As they took the stairs, Beau spoke. "I do not think your mother likes me," she said, in low tones only he could hear.

He frowned, looking down at her. Her expression was not...angry or hurt, exactly. More considering. "What gives you that idea?"

She shook her head and smiled up at him. "I'm sure I just need to get to know her."

"She has been wanting me to get married and solidify my place as leader for quite some time. I'm sure she's quite happy with the situation."

"Wanting you married doesn't mean she likes *me*. Especially if she liked Zia."

Lyon paused as they reached the top of the stairs. He looked at the woman who'd handled the entire evening with aplomb. She looked beautiful. The dark blue of the dress and glittering jewels she wore, along with the tiara, made her look just as a princess should. Elegant and sophisticated.

"You charmed an entire room of people this evening, Beau. Not just people. *Politicians*. Who want me to fail. You charmed them all the same. And you're about to charm most of the country, no doubt. I am very impressed."

The look of concern in her expression slowly changed. Her mouth curved, and a pretty pink appeared on her cheeks. She blushed quite a bit really. Did her cheeks heat with the color? He was tempted to touch, just to find out.

But they had appointments to keep, and it was best if he resisted his urges as much as possible. Control, always. "Mr. Filini, Alice—the head of my public relations team—and the videographer are waiting for us in the library."

She nodded and let him lead her to that room. Mr. Filini bowed. "Your Highnesses. We are ready for you whenever you are. We will have you seated here," Mr. Filini said, gesturing toward two grand chairs that had been placed in front of the fireplace. A fire crackled there, offering a warm glow to the room.

It would come across homey, traditional and steeped in *ancient* history—not the more modern history of a revolving door of his grandmother's brothers' families.

"Here are copies of the announcement we already went through, sir," Alice said, handing a folder to both Lyon and Beau. "Take your time looking it over, and alert Aldo when you are ready to film. He will get the lighting and whatnot ready while you do so."

"You don't have to memorize the remarks," Lyon told Beau as they opened their folders. "This is more of a guide, and my team will edit the video as needed. You'll simply follow my lead."

Beau looked over the paper, clearly concentrating while Aldo moved around them turning on lights, moving them this way and that, conferring with Alice as they looked at the screen. It no longer *felt* cozy, but Lyon knew they would ensure it still looked it on-screen.

"This is very well written," Beau said after a bit.

"I did the bulk of the work, though Alice smooths out my rough edges and we discuss anything that might be problematic. She wanted to be sure you had equal speaking time, so the audience gets the clear impression that this is a partnership. Of you and me. Of Divio and Lille."

Beau nodded. "Yes, that certainly comes across."

"Is there a problem?"

"No. Not at all. I'm just…" She shook her head. "It's strange to talk of Lille as its heir. I still don't feel like it, even though my father made it a reality." Her eyebrows drew together, as if she was thinking through some great problem. "They left without saying goodbye."

She hadn't mentioned her parents' quick departure, and he didn't think she really cared for her parents. Certainly not the way he cared for his mother or had for his grandmother. "Does that bother you?"

"I didn't think it did. It doesn't, exactly." She blew out a breath then fixed him with a smile he could tell was fake. "It doesn't matter. I'm ready when you are."

He wanted to poke more into that little flicker of vulnerability, but it didn't matter. They had pressing things to deal with. How she felt about her parents was really immaterial to him and his life. So he pushed away the desire to get to know her better, and focused on what was required of him.

He indicated to Aldo and Alice that they were ready, and then they began. Alice had them run through the message a few times, assuring both Lyon and Beau she would be able to effortlessly edit the best amalgamation of takes.

But it didn't matter how many times they ran through it, Beau was flawless. When Alice was satisfied, and Aldo was packing up, Lyon turned to his new bride.

"You were perfect. That was practically word for word."

Her smile bloomed. "I told you I have an excellent memory. And I am not prone to exaggeration about my positive attributes, I assure you."

"Perhaps you should exaggerate," he said, and it made her laugh. A low, throaty sound that had his thoughts traveling…elsewhere. Until Alice approached.

"That was perfect. We'll get to work right away and have it posted before the night is over. It will run on the local news program first thing in the morning."

"*Grazie*, Alice."

She curtseyed and then exited the library, leaving Lyon and Beau alone in the room. Cozy and firelit yet again, without a trace of video equipment. He found the strangest sensation of wanting to stay right here. Cozy and warm.

But it was getting late, and he would need to be up early in order to deal with the news response. He pushed himself to his feet, then held out a hand and helped Beau to hers.

Which had them standing close, toe-to-toe, really. She

was short enough she had to tip her head back to meet his gaze.

He should have transferred her hand to his arm. He should have turned and led her to the door.

He counted the flecks of gold in her eyes instead. He let this strange, alluring sensation fill his lungs instead. No, he'd never allowed his reckless urges to win, but this was the first time he felt truly tested. They were alone in his favorite room in the castle, and the firelight made the skin of her shoulders gleam like gold treasure.

He wanted to know what they would feel like under his palms. What more than a brush of lips would feel like. He wanted, and he always denied wants this potent. It could lead nowhere good.

But she didn't move. She watched him with those direct, changeable eyes. She kept her hand in his. If he wasn't imagining it, she even leaned closer. Her breath was definitely coming quicker.

He should have handled this differently. He knew that, even as his mouth touched hers. They needed to approach this with *some* detachment. *Some* rules. Even if a physical relationship ended up being enjoyable, it needed to have boundaries.

Not stolen kisses in a dark library with only the fire in the hearth crackling. While there were much worse ways he could impinge his reputation, he didn't want to be like *any* of the crown princes who'd come before.

Beau melted into him though, before he could pull away. Slowly. Centimeter by centimeter. Small and soft in his arms. He tried to think of the necessary boundaries, but instead the only thing he seemed to be able to do was taste her. Sharp and sweet and addicting, so that for too many moments he took and took and took without regard to anything else.

Because she felt like a secret, this woman in his arms. One he needed to get to the bottom of. A mystery to be solved.

There was something dark and thrilling underneath everything she held on the surface. It pulled at him, spoke to him, whispered desires he couldn't indulge.

Couldn't.

When he pulled back, she blinked her eyes open. Cloudy and seemingly all green in this dim lighting. Her cheeks were pink, and her lips wet. Her breathing coming in short pants.

Something dark and dangerous swirled within him. A want he was very careful to keep deep within where it wouldn't get him into trouble.

She is your wife.

But this was the library. Definitely not the place for *anything* that gripped him. And everything that gripped him was…thorny. Complicated. Not as in control as he needed it to be. He had experienced lust before, identified it and set it aside.

Easily.

This did not feel in the least bit *easy.*

He cleared his throat, so that his voice would sound firm and in control. "I'm afraid your hair looks a bit tousled. And your…lipstick. There's a mirror over here if you want to fix up."

She didn't say anything for ticking moments. Just regarded him with those *eyes* he couldn't seem to read. "Perhaps it would be good for the staff to see me with mussed hair and lipstick. If the goal is to seem like a newlywed couple, that is."

He found himself nodding. She was right. It was smart.

But nothing about the situation he found himself in felt *smart*. Nothing about what was rattling around inside of him was in his control. There was no denying he was attracted to her, that he wanted her.

So instead of *denying it*, he needed to take control of it. It couldn't creep up on him. It couldn't take over so that he forgot everything he was, everything he needed to do. He would never be like the men who'd come before.

Step by step, he'd told her last night. And that was how he'd control this surprising desire.

Step by controlled step.

CHAPTER SIX

BEAU DID NOT know how to parse what had happened in the library. He had kissed her. For no…discernible reason. Except maybe…he'd wanted to?

She had to admit, she hadn't allowed herself to dream about the possibility her arranged husband might actually find her…attractive. The greatest hope she'd allowed herself had been that they could have a partnership built on mutual respect.

It felt downright dangerous to think of anything else, but he'd *kissed* her.

And now he led her down the hall to their bedchamber. *Theirs.* Because once again, they would share a bed tonight. She thought the second night would feel less nerve-racking, but that kiss changed everything.

Everything.

It *hadn't* been a brush of lips. It had been a *kiss*. She had spent a lifetime loving to read a scene about knee-weakening kisses without ever really believing that was a *real* thing, physiologically. But she'd had to lean into him just to stay upright. She hadn't been able to *breathe*.

Kiss? No. Devour? Maybe. Maybe she finally understood that as a descriptor for a kiss. Because…

Wow.

He opened the door to their rooms and gestured her inside. So much of this was like last night. An unwieldy dress she'd need help with. Nerves dancing, but not the kind that created *fear* or panic. No, there was something far more like anticipation wriggling around with nerves.

She felt full of pent-up energy. Like she simply wanted to...*run* or yell or something. So she kept walking, through the sitting room and into the bedchamber. She walked all the way to the large window that looked out over a dark night. The moon hovered at the edge of one of the peaks in the distance, partially shrouded by all that mountain.

She tried to find some sense of calm, some sense of *self* in the celestial scene outside. So they had kissed. So it had been unplanned, and wonderful. So they would have to do a lot more to produce heirs. This was what she'd agreed to. She needed to stop being so silly about it. Romanticizing it. When she'd promised him she didn't have romantic notions.

Because this wasn't romance. It was simply a physical reaction to one another. Besides, chemistry and attraction were good. It would make the whole thing less awkward. And it didn't mean she thought she'd fall in love or get swept off her feet. She was too practical, understood herself too well, had too much to hide to believe in any of that.

So, this was *good*.

Why did it feel so damn scary?

"If all goes well, we will travel to the vacation chalet for the weekend. A honeymoon, in the press. It's up there," he said, coming closer with every word until he was standing next to her and he pointed to the mountains in the distance.

"Is it as beautiful as here?"

"More."

"Then I hope all goes well." She tried to offer him a happy smile, but when she looked up he was gazing at her intently.

"As do I."

Then he didn't say anything. Just stood there. Close and intense. A huge wall of…of…*man*. And for some reason her dress just felt too heavy, too cumbersome, too much. Or maybe it was all of this just too much.

She wasn't sure how to broach the topic, considering what had just occurred in the library, considering the way he was looking at her, but even as off-kilter as she was, she was still *herself*. To the point, no matter the consequences. "I'll need help with my dress again."

His gaze slowly tracked down, from her face and then millimeter by millimeter down her dress, before taking a slow perusal back up to her eyes.

Slowly, his gaze on her, he undid the knot of his tie.

She had no idea why that made her breath catch in her throat, stay there. Particularly when he didn't remove it. Just left it there loose.

"Would you like to have me help you here or in the changing room?"

"My—my clothes are in the closet, so…" She gestured helplessly toward the door, but Lyon didn't move. And neither did she.

"Perhaps we should move on to step three."

For a moment, she didn't understand what he was saying. Then all at once it dawned on her, the memory of last night and him assuring her there would be *steps* to ease them into what they had to do. "Three?" She had to swallow at her suddenly dry throat. "What was two?"

His mouth curved, slowly. *Sensuously.* So that something seemed to curve inside of her in response. A deep, warm *yearning.*

"Step one was simply a brush of mouths. Simple. Something even friends could have shared. Step two was the taste of you."

Taste of you. God.

"Wh-what would step three be?"

He didn't respond right away, but he didn't give the impression that he was somehow thinking it over. No. He knew. He was just…drawing out the moment.

When he finally spoke, each word was carefully delivered in a low, controlled voice. But his eyes… There was something that reminded her of that moment in the chapel. Where despite all his control, all his rigid certainty, she'd seen the flash of something wild.

"I want to see you."

She could feign some ignorance there, but she knew what he meant. Naked. He wanted to see her naked.

Wanted to. She supposed if anything, *that* was the hardest part to reconcile. That these things—the kiss, the *steps* were things he *wanted.* When she'd assumed everything would be…very awkward business. A chore. A responsibility.

This was better. It had to be. Besides, didn't she want the same? "Do I get to see you?"

He lifted a shoulder. "If you wish."

"Well, it only seems fair," she managed to say, not sounding *too* strangled.

The smile on his face was an unfair advantage. The

way he carefully pulled the tie from his collar and placed it across the back of the big, luxurious chair in the corner. Then he turned back to her, considering.

Her breath had completely backed up in her lungs, and it felt as though her face was on fire, while a tension coiled deep inside of her. A heat that centered between her legs. And still it wasn't the anxiety or panic she was used to when faced with an uncomfortable or scary situation.

Lyon moved his finger in a circle, encouraging her to turn around so he could once again deal with the buttons on the back of her dress.

She had to swallow through too many sensations coursing through her before she could manage to get her feet to take the order to move. To turn.

His fingers brushed lightly down the back of her neck. "You make a beautiful princess, Beaugonia. *Beau.*"

She had never been complimented on her looks. She had, in fact, very rarely been complimented. Only Zia ever seemed to see her positive attributes. Beau had thought she was sort of above it. She needed no one else's approval or assurances.

She knew what and who she was. She was almost always certain in her decisions. But that compliment felt… wonderful. She didn't want to depend on anyone else's opinion of her. Didn't want to be some sad version of her mother, twisting herself just to make everything easy. Just to be *approved of.*

But him thinking she was beautiful, or at least saying it, sent a new wave of satisfaction through her.

"I'm certainly glad you think so," she managed to return, without jumping at the contact of his hand on her neck, then back, then at the top button. She could feel his breath dance across her skin. It seemed an interminable stretch of minutes as the dress gently pulled and then began to sag.

She didn't hold it up this time. Even though the idea of baring herself to him made her shake, she kept her hands firmly at her side. Even as the dress slid down, though it stopped at her hips. She could feel him tug it down over.

So the only things she was wearing were underwear and a pair of stockings. Her dress in a heap at her feet. She focused on breathing evenly, just like she tried to do when she felt a panic attack creeping up. Careful, numbered inhales. Slow, controlled exhales.

It was just bodies. Just…inevitabilities. Better to get it over with, wasn't that always her motto?

"Step out," Lyon said. She couldn't quite ascertain what his voice sounded like. Tense, maybe. Still, she followed instructions.

She didn't turn to face him though. She couldn't quite bring herself to.

"Turn around, Beau."

She wanted to make some quip about him needing to say *please* or something about not liking being ordered around. But in this strange, not-herself-at-all moment, she found being obedient was *exactly* what she wanted. It felt like a safety blanket. Something she couldn't do wrong. So she turned.

He muttered something in Italian, but she was pretty sure it was a *good* something, based on the intent glint in his eyes. The way it hit her like its own force, a flame. Her skin felt tight, and she wanted to shake but she wouldn't let herself. She held his gaze. She stood tall and proud.

Even as the air felt cool on her skin. Even as she felt hot from the inside out. Even as she felt the need to clench her legs together just to ease some of the wild tension stitching itself tightly within her.

How did she protect herself from this? From all these physical responses. Chemistry. Attraction. Desire. Whatever word, it didn't really matter. She had to find some way to survive it.

"I think it's your turn," she managed to say. Because this wasn't just her. It was both of them. Stuck in this strange place the world and their own stubbornness had landed them in.

She should enjoy it. Whatever pieces of it she could.

He inclined his head then undid his cuff links, set them in his meticulous way on a little dish on the end table. Then he unbuttoned his shirt in quick efficient moves. He shrugged out of the shirt, laid it across the tie on the chair. The entire time, his gaze never left her body. Like he was drinking in every detail, memorizing it, and everywhere his gaze landed she felt branded. Like every inch of her skin was made specifically for him to see.

To touch.

But he didn't touch. He stayed just out of reach as he unbuttoned and unzipped his pants. So that they stood there, in little to nothing, simply watching each other.

Strangers.

Husband and wife.

She had certainly never been in a room before with a man in his underwear. While she stood there, naked from the waist up. And if she'd dreamed of a scenario like this, she would have included some touching. Kissing. A *bed* maybe, instead of all this standing. Staring. *Breathing* like they were running marathons.

But there was something exhilarating about it. The anticipation. The wait. The soaking it all in.

"The tiara is an excellent touch," he finally said, breaking that silence that had been building like some kind of crescendo in a symphony.

She lifted a hand. She'd completely forgotten it was still pinned to her hair.

"Leave it," he ordered sharply when she moved to pull out a pin.

He had never spoken to her like that before—with a hint of some...*edge*. It heated through her bloodstream like a shot of alcohol. If he didn't touch her... "Lyon."

But something changed. He stepped back. That intense look shuttered. "I think that should be enough for tonight, *tesoruccia*."

She could only stare at him. Enough? But she was... she was *throbbing*. She was *naked*, mostly. And he was near enough. He hadn't even touched her.

"Go get dressed for sleep. Step four will come soon enough."

Step four? What if she wanted *step four* now? What if she wanted to be touched?

But he'd turned his back on her, and all those soaring feelings, all those hopes, deflated. She knew she hadn't done anything wrong. He'd liked what he'd seen initially, so what would have changed? Nothing to do with her. Whatever it was came from him, internally.

And even though her new hopes might include an interesting and enjoyable physical relationship with Lyon while trying to produce heirs, she certainly wasn't foolish enough to think there would be some…emotional one.

So she went and got dressed for bed. Just as he'd told her to do. And if she felt a bit like crying, she doubted it would be the last time.

Lyon did not allow himself mistakes. If one crept on him, he immediately corrected it.

Which was why he'd ended things where he'd ended them. To prove he could. To correct the mistake of thinking he could somehow wield this thing inside of him in a productive way.

If he spent another uncomfortable, sleepless night in bed with his wife, this was punishment for allowing himself to step too close to that edge. Where he focused more on *want* than right.

And, oh, how he'd *wanted*. She was beautiful. Soft and golden. Like some kind of angel. Celestially made just for him. For him to want. For him to have.

But no. That was not his lot in life. His one and only job was to protect Divio. To stabilize it. To *fix* it. The men who'd come before him had hurt Divio over and over again—financially, in worldly reputation and most importantly in breaking the trust between the monarchy and the citizens.

The princes who'd come before had put their own selfish desires first and their citizens last. His grandmother had always made sure he understood that, and that it was his role to be their opposite. To *earn* and *keep* their trust. To pay the debt her family had carved deep.

So he had ended things without touching Beau, though it had felt a bit like cutting off his own limbs in the moment. But he'd done it. *He* was in control. Not desire, no matter how big and hot and uncontrollable the flame inside had seemed, *he* had stopped it.

He was not like his cousins, his uncles, his great-uncles, letting his wants rule the day and ruining the reputation and good standing of the monarchy. He was everything his grandmother and mother had built him to be. A crown prince. The last hope of his family and country.

When he finally took Beau to bed, he would be in control, not desperate. There would be no sordid stories, no pictures, no *whispers*.

He had a certain amount of privacy and freedom at the royal chalet. Particularly if he did not bring any staff. He would work out any…control issues there. When they returned to the castle, he would know how to handle his alluring bride. In all the ways his grandmother's oldest brother never had. *He* had scandalized a country with sordid stories about the wild life he'd led with his wife, the princess.

It had been the beginning of a long line of men who'd behaved worse and more selfishly with each pass of the baton.

Beau tossed and turned next to him, sometimes asleep, sometimes not. He dared not think about what she might be feeling, wanting. It didn't matter. He lay there and watched the gap in the curtains, until dark became light and he could feasibly get up and prepare for the day ahead.

He showered, dressed, then made his way down to his office where he called on a variety of staff members to determine the next steps. Alice assured him the video was well received, which allowed him to make arrangements for a weekend trip to the chalet.

Once he was satisfied everything would run well without him, he began to gather the things he'd want to bring with him in case of emergency. Including the romance novel Beau had picked out yesterday morning.

Which was when his mother walked in. Unannounced.

He didn't bother to chastise her for it. "I am on my way out, Mother. Did you need anything from me before Beau and I leave for the chalet?"

"That is what I came to speak to you about. I'm not sure jetting off on a honeymoon is best."

"I am hardly jetting off, Mother. We are simply going to the chalet. I'm even going to drive." He slid his laptop into his bag next to Beau's book. "A short, cozy honeymoon. It is what the people expect of a happily married couple."

"Are you sure you want time away when people could be conjuring up all sorts of stories about *her*?"

Lyon stopped what he was doing and looked up at his mother. Her expression was uncharacteristically pinched, and there was no missing the disdainful way she had said *her*.

He considered what Beau had said last night. That his mother did not like her. She had not been wrong. And what a good quality for a princess, to know when she wasn't liked, and not react much to it.

But he didn't know what to do with his mother. They had almost always got on. Their goals had always been aligned. Grandmother had passed that goal down to them. It had always been a family tie, and it had always been held with accord.

Perhaps if he thought hard on it, there'd been times as a boy he had felt…chained to his grandmother and mother's vision for him, but he'd been but a child. He could hardly remember those times. Didn't like to. Wouldn't have if his mother wasn't standing here concerned with Beau and *stories*.

When if there was any real concern, his staff would have informed *him*, not his mother.

"If someone finds something that I did not, then I suppose we will deal with it as we can. But I find that eventuality nearly impossible as I was very thorough in investigating the Rendalls."

"The Rendalls. Not her specifically."

"Mother."

"I don't trust her."

While he often listened to his mother's opinions of people, he found he could not take this one on board. She was good at understanding motivations, particularly of the political set. She knew how to handle threats, but Beau was not a threat. She was…

Well, she wasn't a threat.

"You do not need to, Mother. But you need to trust me. And treat your crown princess with respect."

Mother's expression went cool. "Very well, *Your Highness*." Then she swept out of the room.

Lyon sighed. He did not have time to smooth over things with his mother. Besides, she was the one acting out of turn.

She was just worked up about change, no doubt. Just because it was a necessary change they'd both agreed on likely didn't mean it was easy to realize she was no longer needed as his partner. Beau would take that role.

Beau. Likely still asleep. Cheeks flushed from the warmth of the bed, hair tousled from tossing and turning. She'd worn rather unattractive pajamas to bed last night, but that hadn't erased the memory of her standing before him in nothing but—

He shoved the last of his things in his bag. Forcefully. Before marching out of his office. He simply wouldn't think of it. He'd pretend it had been a dream he'd had. Even if she tried to bring it up, he would refuse.

He let that certainty take him all the way upstairs and into his rooms. He expected to find her still in bed, but she was dressed, seated on a chair in the sitting room. She was reading a book, a cup of coffee in one hand.

She looked up. Briefly. "Good morning," she offered pleasantly.

"Good morning," he returned. Then he waited. But whatever he was waiting for did not materialize. She went right back to her book and sipping her coffee. She was dressed perfectly in another pair of dark, loose slacks that looked like silk, and a more formfitting sweater. Today the color of ripe berries.

Which reminded him of…

"Our video has been well received," he said, stiffly and suddenly even to his own ears. "It even got picked up by a few European news affiliates. People are enamored with the story. So, we will head off this morning. I have much to do, and I don't like to be too far away for long, but we will take the weekend as a honeymoon of sorts."

After a moment, she set the book aside—his family biography that he'd given her, he realized—then she looked up at him. Her hazel eyes were a storm of things he couldn't name. She sipped from her cup, then nodded. "Do I need to pack?"

"My staff will take care of everything you'll need."

"Naturally." She got to her feet. "Are we leaving now?"

"In about fifteen minutes."

She nodded. "If you don't mind, I'd like to grab a few books from the library."

"Of course." But he found himself rooted to the spot, blocking her exit from the room. "I have requested next to no staff for this trip. There will be some security, but we will have the chalet to ourselves. Complete privacy."

Her gaze didn't falter, but she tilted her head to one side. Studying him. "For step four?"

He still wasn't sure whether he was delighted by her directness, or if he disliked it entirely. He never quite expected it from her because she was timid in so many other ways. So it continually surprised him, when he was no fan of surprises.

Yet he always found himself smiling anyway.

"For as many steps as you'd like, *tesoruccia*."

"What does that mean? *Tesoruccia*. I keep meaning to look it up."

He wasn't sure why he hesitated. He wasn't *embarrassed* or he wouldn't call her that. "Treasure," he offered.

She laughed.

"Is that funny?"

"The idea that I'm some kind of prize? Yes. Never in my life has anyone…" She trailed off and shook her head. For all her attempts at elegant dismissiveness, a shell of sorts as if nothing got to her, any time she spoke of her family some little hint of vulnerability snuck through.

And reached inside of him like a barb, stuck there, until he did something to smooth it away.

"The truth of the matter is, whatever it is that Zia has done that you do not wish to divulge, it is clear she wasn't going to marry me. The fact you stepped into her place is of great value to me, Beau."

She blinked at that, something soft and sweet in her expression. "I think the only person in my entire life who's ever felt that way is Zia."

"I suppose it is a good thing you ended up married to me then."

Her smile was small, shy. It made warmth bloom in his chest like it was some great feat to make that happen.

So he moved out of the way. So she could go get her books. And he could...figure out what the hell he was feeling.

CHAPTER SEVEN

BEAU WAS SURPRISED when Lyon led her to a heavy-duty Jeep vehicle, and then *he* got into the driver's side himself. She stood there for a moment, simply staring. Until he looked over at her and raised a brow.

"Do princes not drive in Lille?"

"My father said it was beneath us."

Lyon shook his head. "Your father does not improve no matter what more I know about him."

"No, I cannot imagine he ever will."

"Well, we shall get you some lessons when it's appropriate. As for today, I will drive us up to the chalet. We still have some security measures in place, so no worries there. Come now. Let us be off."

With halting steps, Beau made her way to the passenger side where one of Lyon's attendants waited with the door open. He helped her up and in, then closed the door. Once she was buckled in, Lyon started the engine and began to drive.

Drive. "I don't think I've ever been in the front seat of a car before," Beau said. It was a strange feeling, and stranger still realizing just how odd her life was that she was almost twenty-five and had never ridden in the front of a car.

"It is a day of firsts then," Lyon said. He seemed re-laxed behind the wheel, driving this industrial-sized monster.

Beau felt tense. She was determined *not* to be, and thought she'd been handling herself quite well. She had let him be her guide. He had not mentioned last night, so she hadn't. He had mentioned the complete privacy at the chalet, so she had brought up *steps* to indicate she understood what was still expected of her. Even if she didn't understand him or his actions.

She had let his staff pack for her, and she'd only grabbed a few books hoping to have some reading time.

She was being the exact thing she'd promised him she'd be. Easy. Respectable. Flexible.

But she found she really, *really* didn't like riding in the front seat as the roads narrowed and began to twist—up and around the mountains that had been so pretty from a distance, and now looked more and more menacing.

"As I said, we will have almost no staff," Lyon said casually, like he wasn't navigating a giant hunk of metal around roads certainly not meant for something of its size. "I typically like to use a trip to the chalet as a kind of…reset. A reminder I can and will do things on my own when it serves. Do you know how to cook?"

Beau hung onto every word, because it helped her not think about hurtling off the side of the mountain. "In theory."

"How does one know how to cook in theory?"

"I've read a lot about it, but I wasn't allowed in the kitchens. I should definitely like to try to put what I've learned into practice though." She frowned at his large, capable hands on the wheel. "I have less interest in driving."

"Why?"

"Don't you feel…out of control?"

"On the contrary. I feel very in control. I am the one driving the vehicle."

He certainly looked and sounded it. "But the weather, other people, traffic laws and etiquette." She felt a little band of anxiety around her lungs at just the thought.

He spared her a quick glance, with a bemused expression. "Perhaps we will stick to cooking."

She nodded emphatically. "I think that is good." When silence settled again, and looming mountains threatened to cause her to venture into the kind of panic she could not let Lyon see, she scrambled to talk. About anything.

"While I don't have many day-to-day skills, I'm happy to learn them. I pick things up very easily." She kept her eyes on his face instead of the world around them. "I'm very good at math. Exceptional with computers. You wouldn't believe the things I got around my father's IT team's pathetic excuse for internet security."

His mouth curved. "You are a constant surprise, Beau."

"I have heard that before. It's never a compliment."

"It wasn't an insult."

"But it wasn't a compliment."

He didn't argue with her, but the bemused expression didn't leave his face. Perhaps he hadn't *meant* it as an insult, even if it wasn't a compliment. That would still be a novelty in her life.

"It will be a few hours. The drive is quite beautiful though. Especially as we get up into the higher elevations where there's more consistent snow." He glanced over at her and must have read something in her expression.

"You could always nap if you'd like."

"Yes. I think I'll try that." She immediately closed her eyes. She knew she wouldn't sleep, but surely it was better than watching. And if she closed her eyes, she could picture him as he'd been last night. Shirtless. Tall and broad and...strong. Not bulky, but there was something about the way he held himself, something about the shape of him that left no doubt that he could...do all sorts of interesting things with those muscles.

Which left her mind skipping ahead to tonight. And then drifting back to last night. Why had he stopped? Without even *touching* her. Not one kiss while they'd both been nearly naked. It didn't make any sense.

Should she ask him about it? Demand to know what he was thinking? Would that make him angry? Should she just keep her mouth shut and do whatever he told her to do?

This was really not the line of thinking that would help with her anxiety. Particularly since she had some concerns about this trip. Not the privacy because of *steps*, or even that he might pull back from her once again, but because in a smaller place, with less people, it would be harder to hide if she had a panic attack. There was no rhyme or reason for why one hit, though they had gotten less frequent the past few years as she'd learned, thanks to reading books and even medical studies on the topic, coping mechanisms and different ways to keep her mind busy when it wanted to spiral out into anxiety.

She still often had attacks when she faced off with her father, as she had just a few days ago when they'd been visiting Zia at Cristhian's house. She was counting on that meaning another unexplained one didn't pop up for another few weeks at least.

But if she kept thinking about it, worrying about it, no doubt she'd work herself up. So she needed to focus on something else besides this *chalet*. And while she'd like to consider and perhaps discuss what had happened last night, and what would happen tonight, she wasn't sure that was the best *driving* conversation.

Or you're a coward.

That too.

So, she decided the next best thing was to deal with other eventualities. The important ones they'd already agreed upon. She wasn't going to *sleep*, so she might as well prod.

"I was reading your family biography, but it doesn't mention much about your father."

"He was not from Divio, and the book is focused on the royal lines of Divio."

She supposed that made sense, but the two short lines about his entire life had made her feel almost sorry for the man. "Do you remember him?"

Lyon didn't even pause. "No."

As she'd expected. She'd done the math and Lyon's father had died when he'd only been two. His grand-father had died before he'd been born. But he did have a slew of uncles and great-uncles and older cousins. All who'd filtered through the role of crown prince in quick succession.

She knew this was the reason he held himself to high standards. So he would not ruin his time as prince. But what she did not know was if anyone had been a *father* to him. Because certainly no one had been a *father* to her.

"Since your grandfather was also passed by the time you were born, did any of your uncles or anyone fulfill some kind of father figure role?"

His eyebrows drew together and he spared her a look—which she didn't appreciate considering the narrow road. "Is there a point to this odd line of questioning, Beau?"

"I'm thinking about children." Because that was her end goal. Those heirs Lyon needed. Lives she wanted to guide. "You see, I did not have very good examples of parents. Mother or father, but I feel like the bad example is an example in a way. A blueprint of what not to do. But you have nothing."

"What a kind way of putting it," he said dryly.

She winced. "I apologize. I only meant…"

"That I have no example of what a father is meant to be, one way or another." This time his tone was not dry, it was simply flat.

"Well…" She knew that wasn't a kind way of putting any of it, but it *was* true. How else could she put it?

"I had my grandmother and my mother. They were both incredibly strong role models for a young man and impressed upon me the importance of my role. They knew, long before I did, that Divio would eventually come to me."

"How could they know that? So many came before you."

"My grandmother's brothers were fools at best. Their children worse, and so on. Every single male heir from then on either died young, got into far too much trouble before they ascended the throne, or caused so much uproar they had to abdicate to the next. My grandmother always knew it would be me or complete revolution."

What a strange responsibility to put on your grandson. Even if she'd had little faith in the male heirs, it still seemed a stretch to prepare Lyon from *childhood* to potentially take over. But she supposed that was what made him good at his role. What he'd learned. That responsibility that had been pressed upon him.

One that made the word *revolution* sound so bitter on his tongue. "You're afraid of that, aren't you? That's why you're so concerned about…optics and stability." What would he think of a wife who became a shaking, crying mess out of nowhere? Not a comforting thought as they climbed higher and higher still.

"Afraid is not the word I would use," he said carefully, navigating a steep curve as if it were nothing.

She was almost entertained in spite of herself by how clearly he didn't like the idea he might be *afraid*.

"It is a concern," he continued. "But I am well-equipped to handle parliament."

She had no doubt he was. He seemed endlessly capable of handling everything.

Even you?

Well, he certainly made her wonder. It wasn't just the aura he had of…leadership. That passed-down royal thing that had skipped her entirely, that he could walk into a room and everyone would look to him to handle whatever problems arose.

But it was the kindness that she was struggling with. Because if he was kind, would he be cruel to her if he knew about her panic attacks? She wanted to believe he would, because that would mean protecting herself.

But kindness meant a little sliver of her mind sometimes thought *what if*.

"Particularly the parliamentary members who enthusiastically cheered on my family members' worst impulses," he continued, his expression growing dark. "They will not do the same with me."

"Why would they do that? Isn't that counterproductive? Don't they want a stable monarch?"

"You would be surprised what men would do for power," he said grimly. "Their goals were not the good of Divio. Their goals were the good of their own pockets and reach. Sometimes that meant a leader too dependent on the drink to do their job, or too busy chasing women to notice that money is not going where it should. It rarely means a leader who is in control."

"What about you?"

"What about me?"

"What do you want if not power? Being crown prince certainly gives you said power. Being a leader in control is just...power."

"Yes, but it is also a responsibility. I will not squander it as my family has before me. I care about my country. I will wield my power only insofar as it serves our citizens. That is my one and always goal."

Beau considered this, and wondered if it was a speech her father would get behind. It certainly *sounded* like him, but only the superficial words. Country first. Responsibility to country. Damn anything that gets in the way—like a frivolous wife and two rebellious children.

But she was not sure her father had ever considered

his role a *responsibility* so much as a right. *His* birthright. What he was *owed*. It was power, and it was his.

In the end, it didn't matter how much Lyon sounded like Father or didn't. She'd said *I do*. She'd made this bed, and she had to lie in it whether Lyon was a monster or not. So far, he was…interesting. Confusing. But not a monster.

"Did it occur to no one to change the law, allowing female heirs to take the role?" Beau suggested, making the mistake of looking outside once more then, shaken by all that *sky* when they were driving on the *ground*, immediately looked down at her lap.

"A resolution has never been brought forward. But I will propose one."

"You will?"

"Once the timing is right. I want stability, and the kingdom to trust me. To trust what the monarchy offers. But not at the cost of moving on with the times. Divio must be a part of the modern world. But one thing at a time. First, we give them that which they have done without for so many years. A respectable, secure leader."

She nodded along with that. It made sense, and underscored the point that Lyon had *plans*. An entire blueprint for the rest of his life. Which now included hers. If she disappointed him, he no doubt had a plan for that too. She would have asked him about that, but the car came to a stop.

Beau gingerly peered out the windshield. She saw very little aside from blue sky and intimidating mountain. Definitely not a chalet. "Why are we stopping? I thought you said the drive was hours? Is something wrong?"

"You are safe, Beau," Lyon said, reaching over and giving her hand a squeeze. "I want to show you something."

Then he did the strangest thing and got out of the car. It appeared they were on the side of the road, not parked in the middle of it, but still this felt decidedly *unsafe*. But her passenger side door opened and he held out a hand to her. "Come."

She wanted to shake her head. She considered refusing. But there was something about Lyon's directives that did not get her back up like just about everyone else in her life trying to tell her what to do. Maybe it was a confidence born of self-assuredness—rather than Father's bluster, Mother's desperation, or Zia's determination to protect Beau at all costs—even when she hadn't needed it.

Self-assuredness was one thing Beau, ironically enough considering her experience with social anxieties and panic attacks, understood quite well.

So, she took Lyon's hand and let him help her out of the car. He wound an arm around her waist as the side of the road here was slippery. But she realized it wasn't the side of the road, it was an entire parking area. And Lyon led her to a little iron gate.

Beyond it was sky and cloud and mountain. Below them, a smattering of little villages. Puffs of smoke. Bits of green and brown and white. A beautiful landscape. It was so idyllic it seemed like a painting. Not quite real, and yet there it all was spread out before her very own eyes.

Her stomach nearly dropped out, but even with that

disorienting vertigo feeling, her heart…it leapt with joy. "Lyon."

"Beautiful, no?"

"I…" She had no words. Particularly when he stood behind her but kept his arm around her waist. Holding her there against him, like a warm, protective wall.

"There is more beauty to be had once the drive is done. I promise, the discomfort is worth the outcome."

She managed to tear her gaze from the villages below to look over her shoulder and up at him. He'd done this to help her. She didn't know what to do with that. How to feel about it. She couldn't say no one had ever helped her. Zia had.

But this was different. He wasn't *protecting* her. He was simply offering her a kindness. Which made her eyes water and her heart soften. Probably ill-advisedly.

But she smiled all the same. "Then I suppose we should finish the drive."

Beau's anxieties had not melted away when she'd seen the pretty overlook as Lyon had hoped, but she made the rest of the drive with a brave face. He supposed that was why he'd stopped. Courage in the face of discomfort deserved a reward, and it would hardly be the last time she was thrust into a situation that made her uncomfortable.

Oftentimes, a kindness was the best and only reward for such responsibilities. At least, he'd always felt so.

Being the ruling couple of the monarchy of Divio would be full of challenges over the next few years. If she faced them all with such determination, they would end up in a very good place.

When they pulled into the gates of the chalet estate,

and he slowed the car, she finally looked out the vehicle windows. She made a soft sound of appreciation.

He was enjoying her reaction. Aside from her fear of the mountainous drive, she seemed delighted with just about everything. He pulled to a stop and got out of the car, then went over to her side. The skeleton staff they kept at the chalet would have unpacked all their things by now, stocked the fridge and whatnot, and left.

So they would be truly alone.

"I've never seen anything so beautiful," she said cheerfully as they walked toward the chalet, arm in arm.

"Are you just saying that because you're happy to be out of the car?"

She laughed. "No," she said. "Though that helps."

"I have been to Lille. It is hardly an eyesore."

"Lille *is* beautiful. But it is about all I've ever seen. There's something about seeing a new kind of beauty. It's exciting."

"I do not understand why you were so sheltered, Beau. All because of a childhood anxiety."

She stiffened a little but kept walking. Spoke easily enough. "I would think you'd understand perfectly. My father felt he could not risk being seen as weak, and a daughter who did not behave as she should, a daughter who was shy or terrified is certainly a weakness."

He frowned at her description of what he should understand. He paused in front of the door, looked down at her. "I do not need to be seen as *strong*, Beau. That is not the same as stable. As…dependable."

She studied him, her eyes going dark, the gold and green barely visible even out here in all this sunlight. Everything about her was suddenly very serious.

"Could your country depend on a princess who cried if the crowd was too big? Who shook like a leaf if required to speak to a group of people she did not know and feel comfortable with?"

Of course that would be…a problem. A challenge to be overcome, certainly. But it was also irrelevant. "But that isn't you any longer. I know, because I saw you at that dinner last night. You were wonderful."

"Yes, I can handle a crowd these days," she said, her gaze sliding away from his. She gestured at the door. "Aren't you going to show me the chalet?"

He didn't care for the change in topic. This seemed more important, but why would it be? She clearly didn't suffer those old anxieties. She dealt with the wedding, his staff, the dinner and video all with aplomb. Even her nerves over the car ride she had handled very well.

He knew the difference between being riddled with anxiety and being able to handle it.

So this was all…moot. He opened the front door to the chalet and gestured her inside. It was a huge, open airy space, with almost all rooms pouring into each other on the lower level. There were ample windows to see all that natural beauty from, fireplaces in every room and plenty of cozy furniture and warm throw blankets for the cold nights.

She moved forward toward the row of windows in the living room that offered a spectacular view of the mountains. She all but pressed her nose to the glass. "My God. I didn't think anything else could be more beautiful than that overlook, but you're right. This is even better."

There were no villages below. Only mountains and valleys, alpine lakes glittering like jewels in the sun. A stunning and breathtaking view. He'd always loved it. Always loved viewing it in privacy. He could not come out here as much as he liked now that he was crown prince. There was too much pressing work at the palace, but every time he came he felt…renewed.

But he'd never shared that with anyone. Always liked this as a *private* oasis. Where he could sort through whatever needed sorting in his mind. But he supposed privacy wasn't something he had anymore. A wife. Children eventually. He would bring them all here and…

Something about the reality of Beau made all those plans he'd had…not change, exactly. Just flesh out. His children would be people, like Beau was a person. They would have their own wills and whims and irrational fears with some unknown combination of genes from him and Beau.

Beau with her hazel eyes and shy smile. Except it wasn't shy right now. She turned to look at him and she was beaming. Beautiful. But he stayed where he was, by the entrance and out of reach, because he did not trust any of the unwieldy storms clattering around inside of him. The desire, not just to put his mouth on her. To see every inch of her. To touch, to take, *finally* take. That he could deal with. Understandable and all that.

It was the desire to hold her just as he had at the overlook. And feel a strange peace he'd never known, never expected to exist. There was something about the way she *beamed* at him that twined a dark *lust* with some kind of incomprehensible soft desire.

And he didn't trust emotions that twisted. That couldn't be worked out. He needed to set it aside until it could be carefully picked apart and put into a careful compartment of the appropriate reaction.

"We should eat something," he said. Inanely.

Some of the joy on her face faded. He didn't know why. And it didn't matter, he told himself. He led her into the kitchen. He heard himself talk. About the sandwiches the staff would have left. About how tomorrow morning they would need to fend for themselves. About everything and anything that kept him from thinking about her.

"Tomorrow, we'll go on a hike." Bundled up. Physical exertion. Not alone in the same cabin.

"Sounds lovely."

Silence settled around them again. An awkward, uncomfortable silence. Which was new for them. Everything up to now had been fairly easy. All the moments following him on the edge of making a mistake had included a step back. A reset.

But there was nowhere to go here. Which made this feel like a mistake. They should have stayed at the palace.

He had brought her here to get this over with. To have her away from prying eyes and whispers. To not have to worry about…himself.

But he was worried. He forced himself to eat. Ignored the heavy, oppressive silence. When they were both done, he cleared the table. Beau trailed after him. "I also know how to wash dishes. In theory."

He smiled in spite of all these ugly things roiling around inside of him. She was such an interesting woman.

"Let's put that theory to work." He showed her the dishwasher. He instructed her to rinse dishes, then hand them to him so he could place them inside and he instructed her how to put them in properly so that she could handle this chore if she so chose.

But it put them close. Hip to hip as they worked. He could not pretend she wasn't there. That she smelled like something faintly floral. Just the hint of something he'd need to lean closer to identify.

When she handed him the last dish, he placed it inside and closed the door. He turned to suggest they take an hour or so to read before having some dessert, but no words came out as they stood face-to-face. Close.

And all too well he could picture all that pale skin underneath her clothes. The way color rode high on her cheeks, and her eyes darkened with interest when he'd had very little on himself.

She raised her gaze to meet his. He should lay out how the rest of the night would go. He should set out rules. *Then* they could go to the bedroom. *Then* he could control himself well enough to get this over with in an appropriate, heir-making way.

But she leaned in. With a slight hesitation, she slid her hands up his chest. Locked her arms around his neck.

Why did she fit so well against him? Why did it unravel and dissolve every tenet of discipline that had always come easily to him?

Then she rose to her toes and pressed her mouth to his. Initiating a soft, sweet kiss.

It should be sweet. It should be easy. But it lit a fire inside of him that was none of those things. Because he had never had soft and sweet inside of him. He was made by his blood, and the blood was tainted. A line of royal men who'd never resisted an impulse in their lives.

Grandmother had tried to convince him that he could be stronger, better, but he knew.

What he wanted, what he desired, was just as bad as what had felled the men who'd come before. The only difference between them and him was *control*.

Which had never once been threatened like this. When it *shouldn't* be called into question at all.

Whether she was his wife or not, she was innocent and sheltered. That should be enough to keep his desires on their usual simple leash. Instead he wanted to rip every scrap of clothing off of her, take her roughly, right here against the countertop.

Even as he told himself he *wouldn't*, he drove the kiss deeper.

Hotter.

Rougher.

Until she was pressed up against the island. Until his hands were tangled in her hair once more. He could lift her up onto the countertop and have her. Right here. Right now. This terrible pressure would be gone. The mistake made and done instead of hovering just out of reach. It would be relief. It would be a mistake, but he would fix it.

He could fix it.

Or it would open an insatiable desire he could never stop. Or it would get too dark, too wild, and he would be doomed just like every man in his royal bloodline before him.

Maybe it was in that blood—his uncles and cousins had often been brought to ruin by their unquenchable thirsts—but he would not succumb. He could not allow it.

He pulled away. Set her gently back. To prove that he

could. To prove that he would. Tonight, he would touch her. But…in their bedroom. Appropriately. Carefully. Not with this wild thing whispering dark, lurid suggestions in the *kitchen*.

Except she frowned up at him, her dark eyebrows drawn together as she studied him. As if she could see right through him. "Why do you hold yourself back from me when we both know where this eventually must end up? When it seems…you enjoy it at least a little?"

No, there were times her directness didn't entertain him at all. Because he knew the answer, but he could hardly give it to her.

"I suggested steps for a reason, Beau," he said, trying to sound gentle if scolding. He was afraid his voice just sounded…rough. A clue to everything clawing at him.

"What reason?" she demanded.

She was seriously testing his temper. But he maintained his calm demeanor. Because he was in control. "You are innocent. Sheltered, you said that yourself. Jumping into things… It would be careless. Reckless. Sometimes if proper steps are not taken, miscommunications happen. People believe in feelings that aren't… accurate or suitable."

This did not seem to assuage her. Her eyes snapped with temper. She crossed her arms over her chest. "You think if we have sex I'll just…miraculously fall in love with you on the spot? I'll be so bowled over by the experience, I'll just turn into some mindless ninny desperate for love?"

"No, but…"

"But! But!" Her mouth dropped open in outrage. Her cheeks flushed with temper. And it did not help this roaring thing inside of him. It poked at his own temper. It stirred darker wants than he allowed.

"I do not wish to fight with you," he said. Through gritted teeth.

"Then don't be an idiot," she shot back. Then she blinked, as if she realized what she'd just said. Her expression was torn, clearly.

But she didn't apologize for her little explosion, no matter how contrite she looked. When she *should* apologize.

He told himself that's why he didn't let it go, when he should. When *he* was the one who'd said he didn't want to fight.

"Would you prefer I take you in a maddened rush? Right here? On the kitchen counter where we make our *food*?"

She lifted her chin. "Over this strange back-and-forth? Over you…getting me all worked up and then stepping away all icy and weird? Yes, I'd prefer mad rush over that."

Walk away.

The voice of reason was still there. But it was faint.

And he didn't want to listen. He'd show her, instead. Frighten her. Make her *stop*. She would want to stop once he showed her, and then…then…he could.

So he gave in to the roaring thing inside of him. The wants, desires, the dark, twisting need. He fisted his hand in her hair, holding tight so she couldn't move. So she was at his mercy. His for the taking.

Then he crashed his mouth to hers and *took*. It was rough, demanding. The scrape of teeth, his fist in her hair. He gave her no quarter, offered no gentleness. He only took and took and took until those alarm bells he was usually so good at listening to rang in his head.

He wrenched his mouth away, but he couldn't seem to pull his hands from her hair. He couldn't seem to put distance between himself and the soft warmth of her body pressed up against his.

"There are parts of myself I keep leashed for a reason, *tesoruccia*."

Her gaze was steady, her eyes seemed to glow gold. "You are not a dog, Lyon."

But he felt like one, even as her palm slid over his cheek. Like someone trying to tame the snarling, wild beast that roared within.

"You would be surprised," he said, each word a scrape against the thinnest wall of control he maintained. "The things I want. The things I like. Not suitable for the prince I am, but there all the same."

He managed to unclench his hands, detangle them from her hair. He meant to step back. Surely she'd learned her lesson now.

But she reached out, fisted her own hands in his shirt, and held him close.

CHAPTER EIGHT

BEAU HAD NOT meant to call him an idiot. She had not meant to fight with him. That was not the way a dutiful princess acted.

But if this was the punishment, perhaps she'd fight with him all the time. If the way he kissed her was unsuitable but made her feel alive—for perhaps the first time *ever*—then maybe she wanted all that unsuitable punishment.

She looked at him, hands fisted in his shirt so he did not walk away, and saw something in his eyes she didn't understand, but wanted to. Something in his expression she wanted to soothe. But not with sweet words or gentle touches. She wanted this wild thing he offered.

Because she'd never had wild. She'd never been able to follow an impulse. She had lived in shadows and corners and locked rooms.

Now she had…freedom, and she wanted the recklessness that came with it.

She pulled him closer, so that he had to bend down, then she put her mouth to his ear. "Show me."

He made a sound, something she could only describe as a growl. An electric thrill went through her bloodstream at it. At him reaching out once more. With one hard yank, he pulled her pants over her hips, let them fall to the ground. Then he reached out and simply *ripped* the underwear from her body.

Her breath came out in a gasp. A wild thrill swept through her. This, *this* was that wildness she'd seen in him. A hint of it. *Leashed* as he said. And maybe she should be afraid of that being *un*leashed. Certainly she should be.

Instead, she was intrigued.

Instead, she wanted to see where it all led.

Then he cupped her. His big, rough hand on the most sensitive, vulnerable part of her. With no warning, no preamble, his finger slid deep inside.

She wasn't sure of the sound she made, some kind of keening whimper, while he hissed out a breath that seemed to explode inside of her, like a match to friction. He stroked her, slow but seeming to unerringly find just the spot to turn everything into flame.

"Little Beaugonia, so ripe and sweet." He was touching her, doing miraculous things that made pleasure wave through her, build into something tense and needy. "You don't know what you're getting yourself into. But you want it, don't you?"

She couldn't form words. Her blood seemed to run hot in her veins, her breasts heavy and sensitive. She wanted to fidget, but he didn't let her. She wanted whatever her body was building itself up to, but he didn't let her.

He pulled away. Not the way he had before though. No, instead of that detached, cold look in his eyes, they were alight with fire. His mouth a sensuous curve, full of dark amusement.

He pulled the sweater off of her, then his hands were on her waist and he lifted her, set her on the counter island.

The wild pirate she'd always known was lurking under all those chains. And now he was hers. He would be *hers*.

He jerked her bra down, not off. So her breasts were bared, but not free. He brushed a thumb across her nipple, eliciting another gasp from her, the pleasure shocking because how could there be more? His expression went wicked, and he brushed his thumb, back and forth. Until she was squirming. Until she felt…mindless, desperate. She wanted his hands back on her. She wanted *him* inside of her because it felt like that would only ever be the cure to all this need.

"Lyon," she said breathlessly. Needing…needing…

"Yes, I like the way you say my name. Like you're begging. I'd like to hear you beg, Beaugonia. Beg and beg and beg."

Beg. She did not beg. She did *not*…and yet. All those old determinations she'd always believed of herself seemed so weak in the face of how close she was to some unknown pleasure, some great, big feeling *just* out of reach. The kind of thing she couldn't have brought herself.

It could only come from him.

"Lyon, please."

His laugh was dark, cutting. *Perfect*, because it rumbled through her like its own touch. Then his big hands slid up her thighs, then pulled her legs apart. So she was completely bared to him. On the kitchen counter. He pulled her to the edge, his expression dark and feral.

"My banquet. My feast. Do you taste as sweet as you look?" They were shocking words. Everything about this was *shocking*, and yet… She liked it. The wild rush of it. How she knew she should feel some kind of shame, but she only wanted more.

Then she had it, when he dipped his head between her legs. His big hands holding her thighs wide. His dark head at the most sensitive part of her. The chaotic thrall of sensation whirling through her as he tasted her, devoured her like a feast. She could scarcely catch her breath.

And then it all simply...imploded in on itself. She cried out, pulsing through a climax so all-encompassing it seemed like the world went dark, like every inch of her exploded in pleasure and joy and then simply collapsed.

But he caught her. Still sitting on the counter, she leaned her forehead to his shoulder, struggling to breathe. But not like a panic attack. This didn't grip her like fear.

She was smiling. She wanted to *laugh*.

She wanted more.

"Have you had enough, Beau?" he murmured.

"No. No. Lyon, please... We have to..." She looked up, met his gaze. Every inch of him seemed tense, like he was holding back. She didn't want that.

She wanted all of him. She reached out, undid the buttons of his shirt, pushed the fabric off his shoulders, their eyes holding contact the entire time. She let her hands move over him, study him, learn him. And the whole time, she watched his eyes. His wild pirate eyes grew more fierce, his jaw more tense, the fingers on her waist dug deeper.

She trailed her fingers down his chest, the hard cut of his muscles, the trail of dark hair. Then her fingers found the button of his pants. The zipper. She pushed the fabric of his pants and boxers down as far as she could sitting there on the counter.

She didn't allow herself nerves. Like cooking, like loading a dishwasher, she knew how to do this *in theory*. She'd read about it plenty. She only needed to put it into practice. So she reached out and touched him. Closed her hand over the hard, hot length of him.

She groaned in time with him. She didn't know why it should be a thrill to her, but something about holding him in her hand felt like pleasure spearing through her. And that was what she wanted.

Everything.

"Make me yours, Lyon."

She watched whatever thread of control he'd held on to simply snap.

"Here," he demanded, as if she'd argue.

She wouldn't argue with anything if he made her feel that wild, dizzying climax again. If he was inside of her. If finally, *finally* this all made sense. Who cared *where* as long as it happened.

"It is likely to hurt," he muttered.

She wanted to throw her head back and laugh. She knew that was true, but it felt like nothing could ever hurt her again. Not with all this going on inside of her. A weakness and a strength. A joy and something so beautiful it almost made her want to cry. Likely to hurt? Did it matter?

"Only at first," she assured him.

His gaze held hers, as they breathed in tangled tandem. Even as he entered her, slow, too much inch by breathtaking inch. There was something, not pain exactly, but an expanding. Pressure, too much, too much, and yet not enough. Nothing was enough with him.

She wasn't sure she breathed, but she watched him and he watched her. Until they were one. Until whatever discomfort felt secondary to everything else thrashing against her like a storm.

And then he moved, opening up a new world. A new *universe* that was only the two of them together, and that was a wonderful, beautiful, exhilarating thing. Where nothing else mattered, except the way they fit together, moved together, made each other feel.

Both out of body and so deeply within their bodies it was as if there was nothing else. Not palaces or countries or mountains surrounding them. Just the delicious friction two bodies could create.

Until she was crumbling apart by some great seismic event that threatened to rearrange everything she'd built each forward step on. Because what could possibly come after this?

He kissed down her neck, her chest, then his mouth fused to her breast, until that amazing, stomach-flipping climb started all over again. Up, up, up as his grip on her hips tightened. As that tension coiled again, tightened, burst.

This time, with him. He roared out a release, thrust deep inside.

They leaned into each other, ragged breaths, sweaty bodies. Throbbing with all the pleasure that still hummed between them. Beau sighed into his neck, mouth curved into a smile.

She had bemoaned her fate for much of her life, but it no longer felt quite so stifling if it had brought her to this moment.

There was a ringing in his head, an echoing roar in his ears. She was pliant and warm in his arms. Precious and wonderful.

And he had…behaved a clumsy fool. He had handled this all consumed with such selfish desires and needs, with no thought to his *responsibility*. He didn't even have the words for an apology.

He pulled his pants into place. Looked at her. Rosy and flushed, naked on the kitchen counter. Beautiful and wonderful and this was everything he had not wanted. Everything he should have resisted.

But that was not her fault, though it was tempting to think that considering he'd never been driven to be so reckless before. Still, the fault lay with him. Only weak men blamed others for their own mistakes.

Gingerly, he picked her up off the counter and then carried her through the chalet into his bedroom. He laid her on the bed. He needed to leave her. He needed to… to…

He sank onto the edge of the bed. Sat there, head in his hands. What had he done? What had become of him? How did he fix this mistake?

He heard her move, and then she was behind him, palms on his shoulders. "What's wrong?"

"That was not how it should have gone, Beaugonia."

"Why not?"

How could she even ask that as if she had no idea? He looked at her over his shoulder. "Rough and frenzied in the kitchen? This is not appropriate. This is not what a man in control of himself does." He looked back down at his hands. "It was wrong to treat you like that. Wrong to lose…" He didn't even know what other words there were.

All he knew was he looked at his own hands and saw every man in the royal line who had squandered the responsibility of the crown. For power. For a woman. For fun. All to follow their selfish desires to ruination.

He hadn't ruined anything yet, but this felt like the first step down a slippery slope.

Her palm trailed down his spine. "Lyon. I liked the way you treated me. I liked it, and you did too. If we both enjoyed ourselves, why should you feel badly about it?"

He supposed she had enjoyed it. She wasn't experienced enough to pretend, and even if she was, there was no denying she'd been a willing and animated participant. And still he felt like he'd defiled everything he was supposed to keep respectable and stable.

"I must be in control at all times. I am not like my cousins. My uncles." He could not allow himself to be. Perhaps most of them had made their disgraces with women who were not their wives, over money that was not theirs, but anything that could be leaked to the public could be used against him. His grandmother's brother's wild exploits with his wife might not make waves today, but it had at the time.

And no doubt, the man had known better, known it would. But he had cared more about his own wants than what he owed. Which is what Lyon had just done.

It had to end right here. "I will not be like them." Maybe if she understood that, they could move beyond this…misstep.

But she pressed her mouth to his back. In comfort. Like she understood. Like everything she was and offered could be enough.

"This isn't about countries," she said gently. "Citizens and responsibilities. It's simply what we do in the dark. We're married. And… And it's a requirement. How else are we going to have an heir? I mean, I can lay on my back and think of England if it really makes you feel better, but I like what we did tonight better. Well, I assume I do anyway."

He wanted to *laugh*, and he couldn't for the life of him determine why. This wasn't the least bit funny. "Beau." She didn't understand. He could not let feelings and his own wants outweigh responsibility.

Too many before him had.

There had to be a time and place for things. Not kitchens and whenever the need struck. There needed to be lines uncrossed, boxes things were kept firmly in. Anything that even whispered at personal wants had to be done with control and privacy.

But when he turned to face her, she was the most beautiful, glorious thing he'd ever encountered. She was his *wife*, and they *did* need heirs.

But he would have to find some way to put a wall up around all this…dangerous desire. She would need to get pregnant soon. He'd heard from his mother pregnancy was an uncomfortable, painful experience. Beau wouldn't want him then, wouldn't tempt him then. And then there'd be a child.

It could stand between them and…this.

"Our things should all be unpacked. Perhaps you would like some pajamas," he suggested.

She flopped back onto the mattress and spread her arms wide as she looked up at the ceiling. Perfectly, beautifully naked. So that he found himself stirring again already.

"I think I should like to sleep perfectly naked," she said with a smug smile.

"Beaugonia."

She lifted her head, gave him an arch look. "What?"

It seemed imperative then. That she understand. Above all else. No matter what happened. No matter what he felt or didn't. No matter what he resisted, or how he failed. There was one truth to his entire life he could not let go of.

"My country will always come first. My responsibilities. My control. It is my birthright. The promise I made to my grandmother before she died. Nothing can change that."

She studied him with those eyes that would haunt him until the day he died. Like she simply knew everything, and that was why every color danced there. "I didn't ask you to change, Lyon. I didn't ask you to put me above anything. I didn't ask you for anything."

There was something about the haughty way she said that, the little lick of temper in her voice that allowed him to…relax.

He had failed at keeping his boundaries built with her. This was a mistake, but not fatal. It was here, alone, not at the palace with witnesses. It was early in their marriage, and as she'd said…no countries or responsibilities were expressly harmed.

They had two more days of privacy here. He wanted to return to the palace with every possibility she was pregnant so that he could build back his careful walls of decorum. So…this could be okay. His mistake was not fatal and wouldn't be.

He would get her pregnant. *For* Divio and his family legacy. He could relax, at least for another day or two.

"That isn't precisely true, Beaugonia. You did ask. In fact, I seem to recall you begging."

Her cheeks flushed a beautiful shade of pink, but then she reached across the bed and grabbed a pillow. Then she *threw* it at him.

And the laughter that she brought out in him at the worst moments bubbled free. In spite of himself, she made everything feel like…it would be all right. She was a smart woman. She would understand. She would follow suit.

And all would be well.

CHAPTER NINE

BEAU WOKE UP in a cold sweat. Her breath coming in pants. The world dark around her. A strange bed. A warm man. Her mind whirled with something just out of reach.

But she knew one thing.

It had been years since she'd woken up in the middle of a panic attack. And this was the worst possible moment for this to happen to her again.

She struggled to gulp down a breath, but Lyon didn't stir beside her. So there was still a chance. There was still a chance he didn't wake up and find out.

Would it be so bad?

She eased off the bed, struggling to breathe, struggling to feel her legs well enough to walk. The room was dark, but her vision felt even more off than just that.

Would it be so bad? For Lyon to wake up and see her greatest weakness? Something that was decidedly *not* stable or respectable?

Yes, it would be *so* bad.

She tried to move through the room quietly, relief fighting with everything rioting inside of her. Because Lyon didn't stir, and she managed to make her way to the bathroom without making any loud noises.

With shaking arms and increasing panic, tears already

streaming down her face, she managed to close the door without slamming it.

Then she simply collapsed onto the ground. Shaking and gasping. Cursing *everything* that made her the way she was.

Maybe it was lucky. It had gripped her at a time when she'd been able to slip away and hide. Lyon would not have to know. If it could always be this way, then she would be fine.

She tried to let that thought calm her, but once it started there was usually no going back. The attack had to run its course. But she was lying naked on the bathroom floor and that was ridiculous.

She didn't trust herself to stand with as shaky as she was, but she could crawl across the floor to the closet. She left the lights off and tried. Her limbs shook and she didn't want to make any noise so it was slow going and more pushing herself across the floor than anything else.

Pathetic. Stupid. Crazy.

But those were her father's words, not hers. She understood that panic was simply…what it was. A misfire in her brain. She couldn't control it, and it certainly didn't make her any of the things her father called her.

But something about the night with Lyon, sleeping in his bed, made her feel more a failure than she usually did after a panic attack. Because there was no one to prove wrong. No one to spite.

There was only a man she had to hide this…defect from. And not just to protect Zia anymore, but because… she liked him. This life they were creating. It was the happiest she'd ever been. And maybe that was a low bar, but it was a low bar she was determined to keep reaching.

She made it into the closet. There were clothes of hers in here somewhere. She couldn't trust herself to stand to reach the light, so she just reached out around the walls and tried to find a shelf or drawer or something.

Stop shaking. Stop crying. Breathe, breathe, breathe.

She counted breaths. She ignored the tears. Her hand finally blindly landed on something that felt like fabric. Once she managed to get it over her head, she realized it was not hers. It was too big and baggy, but it seemed like a sweatshirt and that would work, even if it was Lyon's.

She brought her knees to her chest and sat there, as her body shook against her will. But with time, her breathing became easier. The tears stopped. The shaking wouldn't go away for some time, but it would lessen. It usually went quicker when Zia sat with her and talked to her as though it weren't happening. Or even her last one, when Cristhian had sat with her and told her the story of when he'd first met Zia.

Even now, the memory warmed her. Whether Zia knew it or not, Cristhian was desperately in love, and Beau had known in that moment that everything she had done was correct. Allowing Zia the freedom of a life with Cristhian and their children free of the palace rules meant they could build a life of joy. For themselves and each other and their impending twins.

Beau was finally able to breathe deeply for the first time. Whatever caused this panic was not from a place of reason, but she was still *reasonable*. And reminding herself how well her choices and gambles had turned out…helped. At least mentally.

Zia would be happy. And this…*thing* between Beau and Lyon… Lust. Chemistry. But also at least a surface enjoyment of each other. It was better than anything she'd had back home. Maybe she had to hide her panic attacks from Lyon and Divio for the rest of her life, but that was better than being treated like some kind of abomination.

The thought of Lyon finding out and making some proclamation about…stability. It made her want to throw up.

So she wouldn't think on that too deeply. It simply wouldn't happen.

Her shakes were better, her breathing normal. She could return to bed and Lyon would never know.

She crept back into the room. It was still dark, and she heard nothing but steady, even breathing. She let out a slow breath herself to steady her steps, and then moved as quietly as possible to the bed. She eased back in.

Lyon shifted, rolled over. "Is everything all right?" he murmured, clearly still half-asleep.

"Of course. I just got cold." And even though she'd gotten dressed, she still felt iced straight through. But her voice sounded calm, so there was that. "I suppose sleeping naked isn't for alpine chalets."

Then he did something that made tears spring to her eyes. He reached over, pulled her into the heat of his body, tucking the blankets around them. Warmth encased her.

Was this what love felt like?

Don't be an idiot, Beaugonia.

Love—real love, not whatever had twisted inside of her mother to make her bow and scrape to Father—was built on trust. And as much as she *liked* Lyon, liked the way he made her feel inside and outside of the bedroom, she would always be keeping a part of herself hidden, because she couldn't trust him with it.

That could never be love.

Which felt like a very heavy, depressing weight in her chest. And while she rarely had panic attacks back to back, she didn't like the way this made her feel. The way tension was creeping back into her. Her thoughts whirling in a loop.

No, she didn't want that. And the only thing she could think of that would stop it was *him*.

"Lyon?"

"Mm?" He was drifting off into sleep, but she needed… something. And never in her life had she had the opportunity to reach out and take it. She turned in the circle of his warm, strong arms and pressed herself against him.

"Touch me."

She felt the shift from half-asleep to immediately alert, and it soothed something inside of her. This effect they had on each other. The way this want felt wild and free and all-encompassing so nothing else mattered.

She fitted her mouth to his. Relief sliding through her along with the post–panic attack exhaustion when he kissed her back. Everything would be okay. Everything would still be better than she'd had.

He pulled her closer, his hand sliding over her back, the curve of her hip. Till he found bare leg, because she only wore his sweatshirt.

Desire slowly sparkled to life as his fingers brushed her leg, up and under the shirt, until his hand rested at her hip, his mouth taking a sweet tour of hers.

But she couldn't do sweet. Not now when she was so vulnerable.

"Don't be gentle," she said against his mouth. She wanted that wild storm of what they'd had earlier.

His grip tightened, then released. She knew he resisted it, though she didn't understand why he thought this had anything to do with how he led Divio. But she couldn't concern herself with his resistance.

"Please. What we had in the kitchen, *that* is what I need." Beyond thought. Beyond reason. Beyond his precious control.

"This cannot be who we are, Beaugonia."

"Just tonight then. Just tonight. Please, Lyon."

And he gave her just that. She knew it didn't solve anything, didn't change anything. This couldn't be who they were, and he could never fully know who she was. Divio was his guiding star and always would be.

But for tonight, she got everything she wanted.

The next morning, Lyon woke up later than he could ever remember waking. But he did not allow himself to think of last night and why that might be. That was over. A new day had dawned, and it was now time to make all the right decisions.

Beau still slept, the covers heaped around her. She looked peaceful if more unkempt than he might have expected. But he could not allow himself to think of the reasons her hair was tousled, her shoulders bare.

A new day. A new page.

They would eat their breakfast, go on their hike. Maybe spend a late afternoon cozied up to the fire with their books before making, eating and cleaning up dinner together. Then, and only then, would they retire to the bedroom. New desires clearly under his control, and then satiated. So there was every possibility a pregnancy came sooner rather than later.

Which he wouldn't think about now.

He went into the kitchen and decided to put together a breakfast and some snacks for the hike. It was rare he got the opportunity to just *be* in his kitchen. Any kitchen. He liked the process of it. Putting things together, having something come out on the other side that even if it didn't look perfect, might taste well enough, and would certainly do the job of nourishing either way.

When he was nearly done with all his preparations, he heard her approach. He steeled himself for a day where *he* was in control of himself. He turned, pleasant smile pasted on his face.

She was dressed in a good base layer for a hike. She had brushed her hair, but she still looked oddly sleepy. He had slept like a rock, except when she'd woken him.

But he wasn't thinking of that. "Good morning."

"Morning," she offered around a yawn. "Is that breakfast? I'm starving."

"Yes. Have a seat."

She approached the table then sat down as he put a plate in front of her. "I will bring a pack for our hike. Water, snacks, but a good protein-rich breakfast is the best way to keep your strength up if we are to make it the full distance."

"Of course," she replied pleasantly. She did not look at him. She did not bring up last night. She wolfed down her breakfast.

She wasn't making things awkward or uncomfortable,

and yet he did not fully feel like himself. His entire life had been in service of one thing—becoming the kind of man and leader who would step into his station once the knock of fate came to the door. He had never considered anything else.

And now he was considering this strange woman who was only supposed to be a business associate at best.

He forced himself to eat his breakfast even though he tasted nothing. Then, once they were both done and the meal cleaned up, they put on layers for hiking in the cold snow. Beau said nothing about last night, and seemed eager to get started, so they set out.

The day was sunny and bright and beautiful. The trail was not marked. It was one of his own making.

She followed along, and he had to slow his pace because she wanted to stop and look at everything. Every rock, every overlook. She poked at ice and made snowballs.

He was surprised to find himself not the least bit frustrated with her constant stops. It was pleasurable to watch her get such enjoyment out of the most simple things.

"Do you always inspect every little thing when you hike?" he asked when she threw one of her little snowball creations and it landed a little too close to him. He turned and gave her an arched eyebrow to get her to laugh.

She didn't. She didn't even meet his gaze. "I haven't been hiking much. My outdoor time usually consisted of finding a hidden away reading spot in the gardens at home."

Lyon frowned. He'd known she'd been hidden away after a fashion with Zia being the heir and her not, but he hadn't considered how much that might extend to *everything*. He'd simply thought it meant events and whatnot. Not actual...life.

"You were *always* kept in the castle?"

She paused, then focused very steadily on a new small sphere of snow in her palm. She took her time responding, as if considering what to say. "It was my father's belief that if I did not show myself in many places, that no one would ask about me. That as long as Zia sparkled, and it seemed as though I did not exist, no one would connect those childhood...tantrums, as he called them... with the monarchy. So, I spent most of my time in the castle." Then, she hurled her little snowball over the edge of the trail. It landed with no sound at all, everything hushed in the snow.

Something in her expression seemed disappointed, and he did not want to see that, feel it twist inside of him like his own disappointment. So he kept walking. "You seem well-equipped to deal with the world for someone kept so isolated."

"Reading opens worlds, even when you don't have any."

He supposed that was true, but he'd never had to put it into practice quite so starkly. And it made him want to...do something for her. He didn't know what. Whatever he offered her had to fit in with the mold he'd created for the perfect princess. The perfect wife of Divio.

But there were little things, he supposed. "Speaking of, I have begun to read one of your romance novels."

"Have you?"

"Yes. And while the writing is quite skilled and the characters interesting enough, it seems to me the whole thing could be solved twenty pages in if they just sat down and had a mature conversation."

"Perhaps, but how often are we as mature as we'd like to be? How often do humans go through great lengths to avoid difficult conversations? How interesting would it be if every fictional character acted perfectly reasonably and maturely—especially considering we as a species rarely do."

It felt pointed, even though when he turned to face her again she wasn't looking at him. So he kept walking on, until they reached the destination of this trail he'd made. A perfect opening to look out over the chalet below and everything they'd just climbed. The beautiful, ancient mountains all around them. And the perfect weather for everything to sparkle with seeming magic.

Her face broke out into one of those beautiful smiles, just pure, simplistic joy at a beautiful landscape. Her eyes were almost perfectly green up here in all this sky and white, her cheeks and nose flushed.

"How often do you make it up here?" She was looking at the chalet, so he assumed she meant this place in general, not the hike.

"Not often. It's hard to get away. Especially with how things are with parliament. They'll take any excuse to paint me the same as my uncles and cousins."

"That must be a difficult legacy to live down."

He frowned a little. "Duties aren't meant to be *easy*." When he'd been young, and still childish enough to complain about what his grandmother expected of him, he'd always been lectured on his privilege. On the special space he held and how he owed it to the men he'd never met to reclaim their legacy. "My *existence* is a payment of a debt, and so I will pay it."

Beau looked at him, her forehead furrowed, her expression one of confusion. "Why should your existence be a payment of a *debt*?"

"My grandmother would have been an excellent ruler, but she was not allowed. I believe my mother would have been as well, should it have been expected of her."

But the look of confusion never left her face. "So? What has that got to do with you?"

"I am finally the male heir Divio deserved. It should have been my grandmother. So I pay the debt lost."

Still, she looked at him as though he were speaking in Italian instead of English. "None of you can control what sex you were born as. That…makes no sense. It was just… The way things happened. Like Zia being good with crowds when we were young. It's just…the way we are."

Lyon resisted the urge to rub at his chest where an odd tension banded. "I am not explaining it well then. I simply meant that I always knew this would be my responsibility, and that I would meet all challenges."

. "That doesn't make the challenges less difficult, Lyon. A duty can still be…a weight. A struggle. Even if you do it with a glad heart."

No one had ever put it that way. It was strangely… satisfying for someone to acknowledge nothing he did was *easy*. That it was *work* to be everything his grandmother had wanted him to be.

She would have given him that assurance, he believed, if she'd lived long enough to see him crowned. Then he finally would have garnered her approval. He was sure of it.

"I suppose," he agreed, wanting to get away from this uncomfortable topic. The way his short breathing wasn't from hiking, but from that weight in his chest.

"Well, I quite like it up here," Beau said brightly, as if she sensed his need to move on. "Hopefully once we convince parliament of your stability, we can come up here more often."

He could not account for how much he liked the way she said *we*, as though they were a team. A partnership. He had not thought of it quite like that. She was an…aid to something. A tool. He had never expected to *share* responsibility with anyone. The responsibility was his.

You are the only hope of Divio, Lyon. All rests on you.

Him and him alone. But now he had a wife. A partner and no doubt Beau could handle her own weight, and that was…amazing, really.

"You will have to make that drive you hated more often to come up here." He even managed to smile as he teased her.

She wrinkled her nose. "That *is* a great shame."

"You have no fear of any of these ledges," he pointed out, as she got closer than he liked to the edge of an overlook. The view was beautiful, but the results of one wrong move catastrophic.

"I trust my own two feet. I do not trust big burly machines to navigate narrow roads."

He smiled in spite of himself, she was such a funny little thing. "Do you have any other peculiar fears?"

"I don't consider it peculiar at all," she replied, all haughty offense.

It was wrong, surely, how much that tone, that *look* affected him. How immediately it sent a thrill to his sex. A desire that threatened to obscure all those rules he'd set for himself this morning.

He turned on a heel. "We best head back." And he set a quick pace. Perhaps unfairly so. She kept up, but when they returned to the chalet with the afternoon sun beating down on them despite the cold air, she was huffing and puffing. Cheeks and nose red. Eyes watering.

But she didn't seem the least bit put out as he opened the door and gestured her inside.

"I know we have to leave tomorrow, but perhaps we could do a shorter hike before we do in the morning," she said, shrugging out of her first layer of coats. "What a wonderful way to start the day."

He did the same. "If we get up early enough."

"Then I suppose you shouldn't keep me up all night." She smiled at him, a glint of mischief in her eyes that lent themselves toward brown now. But there were hints of green and gold. Hints of other worlds entirely.

Especially when she moved closer, reached out and helped him with his first layer of jackets. Not that he needed her help. But he took it all the same. Particularly when she lifted on her toes and fitted her mouth to his.

Her nose was cold, her mouth was hot. She wrapped herself around him like a vine. Surely it was some kind of spell she put over him, because he did not set her back. He kissed her. Sucked under by the taste of her, the *thrill* of her.

She met every nip with one of her own. She arched against him. Moaned against him. Until there was only the beat of desire. Only the need for *more*.

But there were so many layers between them, and the attempt to start getting through them was enough of a reality check to bring him back to himself. To his control.

They would not do this here. There had to be *lines*. Of respectability. Of correct action.

He wrenched himself away from her. Managed to untangle her arms and put some small but necessary space of air between them. It felt like more of a triumph than he should allow himself to feel. He had still kissed her here. Maybe there was no staff, but there were windows. Maybe there was no public here, but he had to be better. Tomorrow they would be in a crowded castle, and he could perhaps excuse some inappropriate kisses with a *newlywed* phase, but he didn't want to give anyone a reason to look at him and think he couldn't control himself.

To look at him and know how little handle he had on his desires for his wife. Because where would that lead? Thanks to the princes that came before, everyone would wonder.

Beau stood there, panting. Looking at him with a hazy desire mixed heavily with confusion. He wanted his hands on her more than his next breath, but he would not give in. He would not be weak.

Divio was his touchstone. Not *her*. Not *this*.

Then she kneeled before him.

CHAPTER TEN

BEAU THOUGHT HE might stop her, but he only looked down at her with arrested desire. Nerves battled in her chest, but she wanted… She wanted.

For the first time in her life she was getting things she wanted. So she would take until it was all gone. Was she pushing too hard? Maybe. But she had never been good at stepping back when she should.

Why start now?

She reached out and put her palms on his thighs, watching his reaction to her every move. His nostrils flared, his jaw clenched, and those dark, dreamy eyes flashed.

"I also understand *this* in theory," she said, her heart hammering against her chest. Not nerves. Just want. "But I'd like to know in practice." Because even if he'd ended the kiss, even if he was worried about *respectability*, she could see the thick, hard line of his erection against his pants.

He wanted her. She wanted him. And she couldn't understand why he didn't want to indulge. She just had to get through to him, that nothing they did together felt wrong. *Was* wrong. She would take that shame away from him. Bit by bit.

Because it sounded like everyone held him to too high standards. She wouldn't do the same. She wouldn't heap unfair responsibility on him. Not when they were alone. Not when they were newly married and had every reason and right to explore this explosive desire between them.

So she pulled his pants down, freeing the hard, heavy length of him. She used one hand against his thigh for balance, then used the other to touch. Explore. Grasp and stroke.

She leaned forward, her eyes on his. And then she used her mouth. Slow, steady. Watching his face. His gaze hard and hot on where she tasted him. Tension wound through his body, and into his clenched fists. Each gentle glide of her tongue made it harder for him to catch a breath, and it spurred her own.

She was throbbing everywhere. No longer cold at all. Just heat. Just need. And a pulsing, skittering feeling of power, when she'd never had any power before. When every act she'd ever engaged in had been hidden.

But this wasn't. Her need for him. His for her. It was theirs and it was everything. Surely he'd see that. Surely—

With no warning, he jerked her back, and then up to her feet. She did not know if he was angry. She did not know what this was, as he held her there, his eyes a series of dark storms. She wanted to find a way to calm them, to ease them.

"Lyon."

"Go into the bedroom," he said, his voice a rough growl that sent a shower of sparks over her body. "Then and only then, you will remove every last article of clothing."

Relief nearly made her sag, but she swallowed and mustered her strength to do as he said as he released her. Turn. Walk away from him and into the bedroom. A tremor went through her hands as she began to get the rest of her clothes off, but it was not panic shakes.

It was *all* anticipation.

She carefully divested herself of the rest of her clothes. She heard him enter behind her, but before she could turn, he spoke in low, authoritative tones. The kind that made her feel alight with incandescent pleasure.

She could not be wrong if he was telling her what to do.

"Put your hands on the edge of the bed, and then bend over."

She hesitated though, not because she did not want to, but because…

"Now."

There was something about the order, the dominating way he was speaking to her that made every lick of pleasure in her body leap higher, twist deeper. She wanted to do everything he demanded.

So she did. Clutched the edge of the bed and bent over. She didn't know what he would do. Time seemed to stretch out, hazy and lost to anticipation. She tried to hold her breath, but still he did not *do* anything. So she was forced to let out a shuddering exhale.

She was about to look over her shoulder, to see where he was. How far away. Just what was keeping him from *touching* her, but before she could finish the move, he spoke.

"Keep your eyes ahead, Beaugonia."

She swallowed. Her full name in that deep scrape of a

voice made a tremor run through her, then center in re-
verberations at her core. Her entire body was like a throb,
and the dark presence of him lurking behind her like a
portent only made the waiting more and more impossible.

"Lyon." She wanted to beg. If he didn't touch her soon,
she might simply shake apart. She needed an anchor.
She needed him. She needed a focal point for all this
sensation to go.

"I did not tell you to speak, *tesoruccia*. You would do
well to keep that dangerous mouth of yours shut."

But then she felt his hand. His palm slid up her leg,
over the curve of her backside, and then his fingers curled
at her hip. He stood behind her, so close she could feel
the heat emanating off of him.

His free hand slid up her spine, to her shoulder. And
then finally, finally, she felt the blunt edge of him enter
her, a slow, perfect glide. His grip on her hip, her shoulder. Being filled while her fingers clasped her bedsheets.

Finally, everything had a point, a reason. Lyon moving
inside of her, so there was only this. Them. The beautiful passion they created when they came together. A joy
that had her falling over that first wonderful edge with a
little gasp of pleasure on a particularly slow, deep stroke,
her forehead pressed against the mattress.

Then his hand moved. From her shoulder to her neck,
to her hair. His fingers tangled, fisted, until he pulled,
so her chin had to come up off the bed. Sparks of something just at the edge of pain twisting even deeper into
the pleasure of it all. Until she was falling apart, shuddering into a million pieces all over again. And still he
did not stop. He only increased the pace, the madness
of it all. Wilder. More out of control. She was only sen-

sation. Only moans and fevered words of *begging*. For more, for him, for all he was and had.

He let out a wild, savage growl on one last, thunderous thrust, collapsing on top of her, his hands still tangled in her hair.

She struggled to find her breath, to find center and the real world again. She wanted to laugh. She had never believed in fairy tales for *her*, happy endings for *her*, but she was beginning to believe in one.

Finally.

She was his downfall. Everything he'd built himself into being. A strong prince with impeccable morals and control.

She'd stripped them away so easily he now realized he was no better than anyone who'd come before. Because he kept making the same mistake. And it got worse every time. Maybe they'd made it to the bedroom this time, but not before he'd let her kneel before him and take him in her mouth at the *doorway*.

Not before he'd spoken to her in ways he never let himself speak to anyone. Not before he'd taken her rough and harsh with that unquenchable need roaring through him like a disease.

He knew how this ended. It spiraled out. Got wilder and wilder until it became a *whisper*. And then a *story*. Maybe it wasn't as bad as stealing palace funds or wreaking havoc with an affair, but it wasn't *good*.

So, fix it.

He carefully withdrew from her, pushing himself away from the bed. For a moment he just stood there, and she didn't move either. Still gripping the edge of the bed, in this deplorable state he'd put her in.

All for an *orgasm*.

She finally sighed heavily, then pushed herself into a standing position. She shoved her hair out of the way and then had the gall to smile at him. She held out a hand. "Let's lay in bed for a while."

He turned away from her hand, gathered his clothes and put them on. Then he turned to face her. She'd arranged herself on the bed, sheet drawn up. Her expression unreadable.

"Do I have to suffer through another lecture?"

It enraged him, this...haughty disdain for all that he was. But he did not explode. He iced it all out. "You clearly did not understand the first one."

Her eyebrows drew together, and she leaned forward. "Lyon, I do not understand this. You are making the strangest problem out of a quite enjoyable thing. A thing we kind of have to do if you want all those heirs."

"When we return to the castle, we must behave with respectability," he returned, locking all of those dangerous wants and needs away. He was only the crown. Only a leader. Not a man, not really.

Hadn't he always been reminded of that when something he wanted did not align with what his grandmother had envisioned for the crown?

You are the crown.

And he would be. "We must, at all times, put forward a royal face. Decorum in every step. No outward displays of affection. No hint that anything means more to us than our roles as crown prince and princess."

"So, I can't do what we did out there in public. Got

it." She didn't roll her eyes, but somehow gave the impression of it anyway.

"You do not understand the precarious position we are in, though I've explained it to you. You do not understand how rumors and whispers turn into demands. These hedonistic desires will not rule me. I cannot let them control me. I need you to understand that. Because if you cannot…" He trailed off, no threat coming to his mind.

Because she was beautiful and naked in his bed and looking at him with some unreadable expression. Or maybe he didn't want to read it.

But he would find an appropriate punishment. He would have control, and he would not allow her to keep… undermining it.

"So, we must be polite in our own bed?" she asked, each word delivered carefully and devoid of emotion. As though she were asking a real question, not trying to make some *point*. "Just in case someone is listening in?"

"We must behave in any potentially public space with respectability, Beaugonia. Perhaps it will be a moot point. Perhaps you are pregnant even now and we will not have to worry ourselves with these…mistakes."

She blinked at that, then looked down at her stomach as if it hadn't occurred to her.

"Would that make you happy?" she asked quietly.

"Of course. That is the entire point of all this. Enough heirs to ensure stability for centuries to come."

She nodded, though she did not meet his gaze. "Of course," she agreed. *Agreed.*

So he didn't know why her agreement felt sour.

"I apologize then," she said at last. "I will endeavor

to be as hands-off and respectable as you." She smiled thinly at him. "Despite the fact two married people enjoying sex should hardly be some proof that you're as foolish as your uncles and cousins."

Proving she refused to understand. "When you give in to your own selfish wants and desires, you begin a downward spiral. Until you'll excuse anything. All for the sake of a little fleeting pleasure."

"I see." But he could tell from her tone that she didn't see at all.

"I hope this is a lesson you can learn, Beaugonia. Because if you can't…" He hated the words before they were even out of his mouth. Felt them twist like regret deep in his gut. But he had to say them. Drastic desires called for drastic measures. "…we may have to have an arrangement more like you had back in Lille."

"Are you threatening to lock me in a room, Lyon?" she returned, all haughty fire that threatened to stir up that which should be satiated. Damn her.

"I am simply telling you that you will obey my wishes, or you will not have access to me at all," he said through gritted teeth.

"And if I'm not pregnant? If there are, in fact, no heirs yet in the making? What then?"

"I suppose there are more scientific ways to go about the impregnation process. We do not actually have to have sex for you to conceive."

Her mouth fell open. "You cannot be serious."

"It isn't ideal, but if it becomes necessary, we will do it. I will always, *always* do what is necessary. I suggest you accept that before we return to the palace."

And because he did not trust himself to say more without this…devolving into all those wants and desires he had to shove aside, he turned on a heel and left.

CHAPTER ELEVEN

BEAU HAD HALF expected him to order her out of the chalet. Back to the palace and his precious controllable life. But she lay in bed for at least an hour, and he never returned with more ridiculous orders or arguments.

Or an apology.

She'd finally gotten dressed, accepting that he wasn't coming. And it was her own fault. She had believed that no matter what happened, this new life would be better than her old one.

But it was just going to turn into the old one, wasn't it? He'd threatened to lock her away. An old threat. One she should be fully familiar with.

But she hadn't expected it from him, and that made her want to cry. But she'd be damned if she gave him the satisfaction.

She sat in the chair by the window and figured she was already miserable so she might as well call her sister.

"What have you done?" was how Zia answered the phone.

"What needed to be done, of course," Beau returned, trying to sound flippant. "But you may lecture me if you wish." Maybe that would take her mind off of Lyon's threats, and how awfully familiar they were.

There was a beat of silence. "I never lecture."

Beau smiled in spite of herself. "All is well, Zia. I promise. I even…" She looked at the closed door. She couldn't tell Zia everything. So, she stretched the truth. "Lyon's been very kind." Minus a threat or two. "I'm not unhappy. Nor will I be." She wouldn't let herself be. "Everything is well. How is it with you?"

"I am not happy with you."

"Of course not."

Zia grunted in irritation. Then caught Beau up on the past few days. A slight pregnancy scare, but she was healthy if on bed rest now. Cristhian, who had been insisting on marriage, walking that back so that it was up to Zia. She complained about that bitterly, but Beau could read what was really under all that bitterness.

Hurt and fear.

Beau sighed, thinking of what Lyon had said on their hike. About being a payment to a debt. It made Beau very much not like his grandmother, which was ridiculous since she was dead and Lyon was clearly devoted to her memory.

But it also made her realize that his outburst, his threats had come from *somewhere*. And if she didn't quite understand from where, maybe it was the same as Zia.

Hurt and fear.

Could she excuse that his hurt and fear meant if she didn't bend and scrape to what he wanted, she would be locked and hidden away once more? Artificially inseminated into having his heirs, all so he avoided this supposed slippery slope of desire.

Why don't you tell him all about your panic attacks then? That'll really get him going.

But the thought made her sad rather than mad. Because she did not *agree* with him about anything he'd said, but she was beginning to understand it all the same. He believed he had to be…perfect, she supposed. Better than his uncles and cousins.

A responsibility put there by someone he cared about. Not just himself.

"How am I supposed to know what the right choice is?" Zia demanded, pulling Beau out of her thoughts.

But Beau didn't know. Even if she did, Zia had to work it out on her own.

Beau listened and made the appropriate comforting noises. Maybe this was how she needed to deal with Lyon too. Maybe there was no pushing. Maybe he had to come to his own conclusions. Maybe he had to realize on his own that threats were…cruel.

But was that fair, she wondered after hanging up with Zia. He wasn't like her father. There was something noble about what Lyon was trying to do. It wasn't about *his* position, it was about what he felt he owed to his grandmother's memory and his country.

She sat with that for a moment, an uncomfortable worry creeping in. That she was excusing his bad behavior because…because she cared for him.

She rubbed at her chest that suddenly felt too tight. He *wasn't* like Father. That was a fact, not her being blinded by…whatever it was she felt. Not love, no. It was too soon for that. There was still so much they didn't know about each other, and she'd never trust him with her secret.

But there was the chemistry. That was undeniable.

And she enjoyed his company. But why she *liked* him *was* the sense of being…noble or responsible or something. An inherent sense of right and wrong. It made him a good man.

These were facts. Not things she'd convinced herself of because she had feelings for him. And facts were what she should focus on. She reached into her bag and pulled out the boring, dry biography of Lyon's royal line.

Maybe the answers to his…rigidity were in these pages. She skimmed the first few chapters. All ancient bloodlines and wars for "freedom" and "ways of life" which were really only ever about one group having power over another. The history of the world forever.

Eventually she reached his great-grandfather. It seemed he'd been an excellent leader. Loved by all, as his wife had been. His life had been cut rather short by a sudden heart attack, and then the instability had begun.

The next crown prince, his grandmother's eldest brother, it didn't appear had done anything all that wrong. There had been rumors and stories about the prince and princess, and some lurid pictures printed, apparently, but nothing illegal or particularly wrong. He'd died young though. Another heart attack.

The next crown prince, another brother, had held the position for only a year before he'd been forced to abdicate to his brother after it was brought to light he'd been using palace funds to pay off illegal gambling debts.

The next prince had held the position for almost three years—before the grumblings of the female palace staff had become so great they couldn't seem to hire anyone to work at the palace. It didn't take a detective to figure out why.

He'd abdicated, claiming health issues. It went on from there. Sons. Brothers. Each story a little more salacious than the last so that she had to consult the internet to fill in the blanks as the book glossed over the more despicable acts.

A series of prostitutes given free rein and then stealing historical artifacts from the palace. Affairs that ended in public feuds. An inappropriate relationship with an underage woman that would have ended in actual jail time if the prince hadn't "suffered a heart attack."

There were all sorts of internet conspiracy stories about his death.

Yes, Lyon had quite the history of men who couldn't handle themselves or their power stretching out behind him. She didn't understand why the misdeeds of his family would hang around his neck like a noose, but she could see that they did, and why that might have him lash out in all that fear and hurt.

She closed the book and put it away, considering. If he truly believed giving in to anything he desired was a slippery slope to destruction, then perhaps she should not be angry with him.

Or are you turning into your mother?

She scowled at that thought. She was hardly going to twist herself into a pretzel for him, but she had promised him she would be the wife *he* needed. For Zia's future, she had promised to be a picture-perfect princess.

If that meant ignoring chemistry and enjoyment and keeping her distance from her husband who made her feel *alive*, well. That was the deal she'd made, wasn't it?

She blew out a breath, her stomach's growling only growing louder. Loud enough she could no longer ignore it. She finally got up and left the room. Perhaps he'd abandoned her here.

But the minute she left the bedroom she smelled food. She followed the scent to the kitchen. Where he stood over the stove, working on something.

Quite the sight. A handsome prince cooking a meal in his beautiful chalet kitchen. She had no mad left, and it filled her with a certain amount of anxiety. Shouldn't she still be mad? He had threatened to essentially lock her away. She should be furious.

But she found none of her ire watching him cook. Thinking of what he'd said about debts and payments. Bloodlines and respectability.

"It is almost ready," he said without looking at her.

She sighed and settled into a seat at the table. He served them dinner, making no eye contact whatsoever. It was a hearty-looking stew, and warm rolls glistening with butter.

"You've utilized your afternoon wonderfully," she offered, hoping to ease some of the tension choking the air.

He only made a vague agreeing sound before taking a seat at the table.

Beau was half-tempted to say something shocking, just to get a reaction out of him. But that wasn't being a good princess, was it?

So she said nothing. They ate without speaking to one another at all.

It kind of made her want to cry. But she was going to prove to him that she could give him what he wanted. She was going to try, anyway. So, she did everything he did. She helped him clean up the dinner without saying a word. When he retired to their rooms to take a shower, she retired to their rooms and read in the chair until he emerged. Then she silently went into the shower herself. She put on her coziest, baggiest pajamas and returned to the room.

He was already in bed. All the lights off, save one.

The small one by her side of the bed. It was an oddly thoughtful gesture that had tears springing to her eyes. And a horrible thought infiltrating.

She wanted him to care for her. In little ways and small ways. And she worried that it would come at great cost to herself, that want.

So maybe she understood him and his worries after all. She didn't want to be her mother. She'd never once thought she could be.

Until she'd started to develop these soft, caring feelings for him, and sometimes considered putting his own needs before her own. Would that only get worse? Until she too was bowing and scraping to make him happy at the cost of everyone else?

Terrible, *terrible* thought. One that made her cold straight through. But in that cold, she felt even worse for having argued with him earlier.

They really weren't all that different, were they? And his concern about falling into the traps of his family wasn't so outlandish, was it?

But she didn't know how to broach the topic with him. She didn't know how to apologize or make this right. And still, she couldn't stand the silence any longer.

She slid into bed, searching for the right words. "Are we going to awkwardly toss and turn all night or can we discuss the elephant in the room?" Definitely not the right words.

"There is no elephant," he replied gruffly.

She snorted. Hardly. "I accept that you find our... chemistry...appalling."

"I didn't use that word."

"Horrifying?" she asked, because she didn't know how to have a conversation that wasn't her poking at someone. She didn't know how to just be...open and vulnerable.

"It isn't the chemistry itself, Beau. It is how it makes me behave."

She supposed if there was anything she respected about this entirely frustrating and nonsensical thing it was that he blamed himself. Not her. Usually she was the easy target for blame in an argument.

Which didn't help with all this...*softness* in her heart when it came to him. But instead of continuing to think about her mother, she shifted her focus to what she'd learned about relationships. She knew things only in *theory*, but that was something, she supposed.

Mature adults had mature conversations. Just like the ones Lyon bemoaned had been missing from the book he was reading.

"I read about your uncles and your cousins. What the book glossed over, I looked up on the internet."

There was nothing but silence from his side of the bed. She could take that as a sign to stop talking, but she didn't want to return to the palace like this. Or worse, have to fake smiles and conversation for the staff, and then retreat to stony silences when they were alone.

"It helped me understand better, I think. It is quite a lot of bad behavior from one prince to another, and it makes your place all that more…challenging. To prove you are not like them."

It was not in her nature to apologize. She generally thought she was correct in everything she did. But this wasn't actually about being right or wrong. It was about a promise she'd made, and something he felt strongly about.

It was about, like him, the need to do the right thing. It wasn't about caring for him so much she needed to smooth this rift over. It was simply the right thing to do.

"I apologize, Lyon. I…may not agree with everything you've said today, but I understand where it's coming from now."

Lyon did not move. He continued to stare blindly at the darkness in the room. Apologies were a dime a dozen, his grandmother had always made sure he understood *that*.

But the way Beau said hers made him want to…believe her.

"I made a promise to you when we arranged this," she continued. "I would be what you needed. I promised to give you heirs and be a steady, respectable presence for your country. I'll admit, I don't understand why there needs to be such a hard line on decorum when people are meant to believe we're…in love, but I don't need to understand to respect that this is how *you* feel."

He finally rolled over to face her. She was sitting up in the bed, knees drawn to her chest. She was mostly a shadow, but he could tell her hair was free around her shoulders.

There was a humming need to reach out and touch, but he did not indulge himself. If he gave in tonight, not only was he a complete failure to himself, but he would be failing her.

She was apologizing. Saying she understood. He could hardly be the reason that didn't matter.

"My grandmother used to say apologies are pointless. Pretty words meant for the recipient to ignore what can't be fixed," he said, pushing himself into a sitting position like she was.

"That's a rather dire view of apologies. Particularly ones honestly given. Besides, I don't wish you to ignore anything. I'm only…reassuring you that I have not forgotten the promises I made. I can't promise to be perfect, that has *never* been in my nature. But I promise to try."

For a moment, he couldn't find any words. Couldn't understand this. He'd expected icy silences and perhaps another fight before they returned to the palace. He'd expected to have to make good with his threat and keep her as much out of view and away from him as possible.

But she undercut it all. With an *apology*. One that sounded so sincere, he did not know how to ignore it. One that felt like a bridge, past the struggles they were currently facing and toward a mature relationship of mutual understanding.

"No one has ever apologized to me in a way that felt genuine. I have always agreed with my grandmother's estimation. Until this. I accept your apology, Beau. Thank you for understanding."

She inched a little closer. Hesitantly. Until her shoulder pressed to his. He didn't want to push her away. This was a *gesture,* to go with her apology. To bring them back to accord. So he carefully placed his arm around her shoulders. Not pulling her in, but not pushing her away either.

There was a danger here. In the warmth of their bodies comingling, in the sweet, floral scent of her. But there was also a strange, sweet comfort. If they worked through this so early in their marriage, that was an excellent precedent to set for the future.

She leaned her head against his shoulder. "I do not wish to return to the palace at odds."

"Neither do I." He wanted to kiss her then. He wanted the sweet comfort of her body next to his. Under his. "I apologize as well. I should not have resorted to threats. Fights have no place here."

She didn't say anything to that, just sat next to him. He could have stayed right in this moment forever, but even this unknown gentleness felt like the kind of thinking that pulled a man down and under. Perhaps more so than straight desire. Desire was fleeting.

But caring about her... What kind of slippery slope would that be? So he very lightly brushed his mouth against her temple.

"Good night, Beau," he said, then moved over to his side of the bed.

"Good night, Lyon," she returned, moving over to hers.

Just as it should be. Just as it would be.

CHAPTER TWELVE

BEAU HAD SLEPT well enough. She'd woken up the following morning in the middle of the bed, and like happened so often, Lyon was already up and gone. She lay there for a moment, not sure what to do with this strange tide of grief inside of her.

What was there to grieve? They had made amends. They would return to the castle today on the same page. Respectable, stable royals who respected one another, but didn't so much as have one lustful thought.

On a groan, she rolled out of bed and got dressed. When she shuffled out to the kitchen he was already dressed for the day and had made and cleaned up breakfast. Only a covered plate remained on the table, no doubt for her.

Because he was full of small gestures that no one had ever really given her, and she did not know how to reconcile this with a man who'd threaten to lock her away—when he didn't even know her full secret.

But he greeted her with a smile and "good morning." When she sat down to eat, he told her about some bird he'd watched fly around outside the window and surprised her with the idea that it was a good omen.

"You have never once struck me as the superstitious sort."

"Well, I only accept good superstitious."

It made her laugh. And she tried to hold on to that humor, that story as they drove back to the palace. The drive down was not quite as anxiety-inducing as the drive up, but she still didn't enjoy it.

They returned to the castle, a flurry of staff, a sit-down meal with Lyon's mother. Two days away without staff should not have had time to feel like normal, but suddenly all these people and space felt *overwhelming*.

But she knew her role. She smiled through dinner, ignored the countess's backhanded commentary about their *vacation*. She set out to be exactly the princess she had promised Lyon she would be.

Back then, she'd been doing it for Zia. Funny how it felt…different now. Like she was doing it for *him*.

When they retired to their rooms for bed, all the tension she'd felt from the night before seeped back into the silences between them. He wasn't angry, and she wasn't angry, but there was this gulf of not knowing how to be between them.

She wanted to reach out to him. Even if just for a hug. It could be something platonic. Just the feeling they… they…

But he took a gentle sidestep. "I think we should… wait."

"Wait?"

"It is possible you are already pregnant. We should wait to see if that is so."

Every time he said *pregnant*, she had a strange pang deep in her chest. The idea of already growing a child filled her with…a twist of so many different emotions. There was a deep yearning she really hadn't known was there until Zia had become pregnant. Then she'd started corresponding with Lyon about taking Zia's place and he'd made it clear he needed heirs.

She'd started to think of what it meant to be a mother. To care for someone else and show them love in the way her parents never had. She wanted that.

The idea of *love* was also causing strange pangs these days, because when she looked at Lyon, even not wanting to *wait* to see if it was so, she wanted to give him what he wanted. She wanted to find a way to make him happy.

So she hoped she was pregnant. For him just as much as for herself. But she'd also read enough books to know that not everyone got pregnant right away. Though Zia had with Cristhian, so maybe…

But what if she wasn't? They still needed heirs.

And he stood there, distance between them, hands behind his back. Stiff and uncomfortable but set in this decision he'd made. All on his own.

"And if I'm not?"

"Then we will develop a schedule."

"A schedule?"

His mouth firmed, but he didn't get angry. He stayed perfectly calm. If a little sarcastic. "Do I need to explain what a schedule is?"

"No." She looked away, feeling small. Angry she'd let something twist inside of her so that she allowed someone to make her feel small. She had promised herself she'd left that behind when she'd escaped her father's grip.

And now she wasn't just *allowing* it to happen, she

was…wanting to find some way to take that stiffness away that would make him *happy*. That would bring back the *ease* they'd had around each other.

Not just the sex, but the comradery. The feeling there wasn't some invisible box around the both of them.

"There are times when a woman is more…susceptible to getting pregnant, are there not?" Lyon said, when she couldn't come up with any words. "We will develop a schedule based on the best possible time."

She found herself nodding along even though the idea sounded…terrible. A *schedule*. For sex? When they *enjoyed* sex with one another?

She had promised him she understood. She had promised to be the princess he needed. If that meant waiting and schedules… Did it really matter or change anything? It was better than being locked away.

So days passed, and Beau settled into a schedule as crown princess of Divio. She settled into a life. She dined with Lyon, and sometimes the countess. She got to know all the different staff members, started developing projects with her own assistant. She talked to Zia almost every day, even video calling into Zia and Cristhian's wedding.

She had watched over her phone as Cristhian and Zia had made vows to one another, far away in Cristhian's place close to Germany. She had seen the love shine between them even on a small phone screen and had been overjoyed her sister had found it.

Overjoyed they had both found their freedoms. Because this *was* better than the life she'd had in Lille. And if every day she spent more time convincing herself of that…well, it *was* better.

Even if every night she slid into bed with her husband, and he kept his back to her. Even if he never so much as held her hand in public. He was always courteous and kind. He made sure the books she wanted were ordered, the meals she liked served. They talked about books. He read things she suggested and vice versa.

They had developed a friendship. It was better than her wildest dreams of what her life might look like when she'd been locked in her room, the threat of an *institution* hanging over her head.

It was *better*.

For two weeks she convinced herself of that, and then one afternoon when it became clear that she wasn't pregnant, she finally realized the truth.

She was miserable.

"Your Highness?"

Lyon looked from the window to Mr. Filini, who had been talking to him about the upcoming parliamentary dinner. Lyon wasn't sure when his thoughts had strayed. What information he'd missed because he'd been *brooding* about Beau.

It was becoming frustratingly common. He couldn't focus. He couldn't stay in his present moment. Every day he became…more and more uncomfortable.

It wasn't even just the wanting her. Which he still did. With a fire that never truly seemed to go away. But he controlled it. Resisted it. He could almost convince himself he'd conquered it.

But he was worried about Beau, and he didn't even understand why. Everything was just as it should be. Just as they'd agreed.

They'd been back at the castle for nearly two weeks now. It should feel like normal.

But no matter how he tried to ignore it, he missed the way they'd been at the chalet. Even in turmoil that had at least been…real. It hadn't felt like playacting.

But playacting was better than failing everything he'd set out to do. So there was that. Now he just needed to figure out how to resist thoughts of her, what she might doing, what was going on in that fascinating brain of hers when he needed to be focused on the task of ruling a kingdom.

"A list of what you still need to sign off on will be in your email within the hour, sir," Mr. Filini said.

"Thank you," Lyon said. Maybe he hadn't been focusing well, but nothing had slipped through the cracks yet. Everything was going on just as it should. Parliamentary business addressed. The public response to Beau was increasingly positive.

Everything was going just as it should.

And damn it, he couldn't relax.

Perhaps he should talk to Beau. Point-blank ask her what was wrong. Would she stop taking up so much of his brain space if he did? He could fix whatever problem was vexing her, and then it wouldn't feel like his tie and all those old anxieties were choking him by the end of every day.

Unless it was…the lack of intimacy that troubled her. But she'd said she understood that. She'd *apologized* for not initially understanding.

They needed to have a conversation. There was no getting around it. Hadn't he complained of her books avoiding them? Well, he was not a coward. He would ask. She would tell him. He would fix it.

The end.

He strode up to their rooms. She was not in the sitting room or the bedroom, but before he could call out for her, she stepped out of the bathroom.

When she saw him, she smiled, but he could tell she had been crying. He was almost certain of it. Her eyes were red and puffy. He'd never seen her in such a state. His entire being simply...bottomed out.

He strode forward, some horrible feeling gripping him. Like if she wasn't okay, nothing would be. "Is everything all right?"

"Yes, all in all." She tried to keep the smile, but it faltered. "I am... I am not pregnant. Not a tragedy, of course. Just..."

"Ah." It was the most insipid thing to say, but he had no words for this. He wanted to hug her close and take that pain she was trying to hide away, but he couldn't allow himself that.

It *wasn't* a tragedy, she was right, but she clearly was saddened by it, and he wanted to fix it. But there was no...fixing. Not in the moment.

He should be disappointed as well. But for a soaring, blinding moment all he could think was that he would be able to touch her again. He would have the opportunity to stop this deep, rending pain at keeping his distance and have her in his arms. It would be his royal duty once more.

He had been hoping for an heir, or so he told himself. But in this moment he realized what he'd really wanted was the excuse to touch her again.

Because deep down he was selfish. He was a product of the men who'd come before. Driven by only his own wants.

"I have read up on the subject," she continued, moving slightly away from him. "And it's quite commonplace for it to take up to a year even if both parties are perfectly healthy. Particularly for the first child." She peered out the window as if something of great interest existed out there beyond the mountains that always lurked in the distance.

"Yes, that makes sense." Why did he sound so damn stiff?

"In happy news, Zia has had her twins." Her smile was genuine, maybe, but it trembled at the edges. "I should like to plan my visit."

She had told him of Zia's marriage to Cristhian Sterling a few days ago, and that Zia was expecting to have her children any day, and that Beau would need to visit and meet her niece and nephew.

"Of course. I'm afraid we'll need to make it through the parliamentary dinner before you can go, though."

She nodded. "That's all right. I'm sure Zia would like a few days to settle in with her new family."

"We shall visit together," he said, wanting to offer some kind of…something. He didn't have the words, but maybe an action would get across what he was feeling.

"You could get away from Divio?" she asked. Almost like she didn't believe him. But at the same time, he saw something in her expression he hadn't seen in a while. A kind of openness. Maybe even…hope.

"I may not be able to do it right away, but I'll find a

few days. It will be a good look for us. Proof that there are no hard feelings."

Something in her expression shuttered. That blank that was seeping into his bones like worry and fear. An old anxiety that had him loosening his tie in spite of himself.

"Are there no hard feelings?" she asked at length, not meeting his gaze.

He blinked. He had not thought of Zia in ages. Why would he think of her when there was Beau? She occupied nearly all of his thoughts whether he wanted her to or not. "None."

Beau let out a great sigh, her gaze back on the window, making her eyes fairly glow green. Her voice was rough when she spoke. "She would have made you a better wife."

He heard the anguish in that, saw it in her slumped shoulders. He did not understand where any of this had come from, but he could hardly…stand it. He moved over to her, and carefully, lightly touched her chin, nudging it gently up so she would have to look at him.

"You are the best wife I could ask for." Which was just the most basic truth. She tested him, yes, but in all other ways she was better than he could have imagined. She handled the staff perfectly. She didn't wither under his mother's ridiculous commentary. She understood him, and it was…different than everyone else.

His mother understood him, but she depended on him. To uphold the name, the kingdom, her bloodline. Beau understood him to…support him. She had acknowledged his place could be difficult. She…

Didn't she understand that? Apparently not because

LORRAINE HALL   151

her eyebrows drew together and she studied him with eyes still shiny from her earlier tears.

He hoped they were her earlier tears.

Then she looked away, pulling her chin away from his touch. "Would it look unseemly if I missed dinner tonight?"

Lyon had no idea how to fix this. Except to give her whatever she wanted that he was able. This was one of those things.

"No, of course not. There are no events scheduled. I'll make sure a meal is brought up."

She nodded.

More of that oppressive silence he didn't know what to do with, so he made a move to leave. Not sure why that felt so dissatisfactory.

"Lyon?"

He stopped, turning back to face her, even if she wasn't looking at him.

"Do I make you happy?"

Happy was not what he felt. Happy seemed simple, and nothing about what she did to him, what was rioting through him was *happy*. But it was…good. Positive. She was a positive in his life. So he nodded. "Yes, Beau. Very happy."

Her mouth curved then. He could hardly call it a smile, but it was better than bleak and blank and all the ways it had felt like she was withering before his eyes.

"All right then," she said with a nod. "If you'll have Mr. Filini forward me a copy of the etiquette document guests receive for the parliamentary dinner, I'll go over it with my dinner."

"You have the one for the crown princess."

"Yes, but I'd like to understand what's expected of the guests as well. What they see, so I can make sure I can put them at ease in whatever ways I can."

"You don't have to do all that."

"I'd like to," she said firmly.

"All right. Well. It will be done then."

"Excellent."

Then they stared at each other. She said nothing. He didn't have the first clue what to say. So…he left.

CHAPTER THIRTEEN

BEAU COULD NOT pretend she was happy. Misery seemed to seep into every corner of her life. Every moment felt like more of a chore than it should. She tried to maintain a positive outlook on everything, but the only thing that made her even feel remotely happy and alive was video calling with Zia and the twins and reading the most outrageous books she could find. Dragons and alternate universes. Time travel and postapocalyptic worlds that allowed her to forget all about her very boring world.

A world where she felt increasingly in love with her husband, and increasingly miserable for it. Even though she'd only had one panic attack since the one at the chalet, and she'd hidden it easily, she couldn't even be happy about that. She was living in a world where she did everything she swore she'd never do.

Bend and twist and hide in an effort to make a man happy.

All because he'd said she was the best wife he could ask for. All because he'd said she made him happy. Day in and day out, no matter how many nights she spent chastising herself, she twisted herself into a more miserable pretzel because making him happy felt like...like...

Oh, she didn't know, so after she finished up her usual

morning call with Zia, she picked up a book about a young woman who went through a portal to a land full of dragons, fairies and evil. It was far better than wondering if her husband was ever going to touch her again for those heirs he claimed to need.

The countess chose this moment to sweep into the library, the usual disapproval in every line of her face. Beau wanted to groan aloud.

"Well," she sniffed. "It must be nice to *relax* when the entire palace is readying itself for tomorrow's dinner."

Beau smiled as she always did. Not out of politeness, but because when she didn't bristle it only seemed to make the countess more angry.

Well, at least she hadn't *completely* lost herself.

"What a welcome interruption then," Beau said brightly. "I was under the impression I had prepared in every way possible, but is there something you think I've missed?"

The countess sniffed. "*I* would be ensuring that I knew everything I was supposed to know, backward and forward. Not reading…filth."

"Ah, well, I'm afraid I *do* know everything backward and forward. So filth it is."

The countess scoffed, which scraped against Beau's last nerve. She hated for her intelligence to be insulted. She hated the way the countess was always harping on her to do things differently. No wonder Lyon was obsessed with control and doing the right thing.

The woman who'd raised him was *equally* obsessed, if not more so. Then if she added in stories of his grandmother, well, she understood why they were all such… external perfectionists and internal messes.

"Quiz me then," Beau said, barely resisting tossing her book down like a gauntlet thrown.

"I beg your pardon?"

"If you do not think I have the knowledge to handle this event, quiz me." She kept the fake smile firmly in place. "I would love to show you just how prepared I am."

"That is no way to talk to me, young lady."

Beau happened to think she was being very calm, but there was no point arguing with someone who wanted her to be at fault. "I apologize. I only meant that I'd be happy to prove to you that I am quite ready so you needn't worry so."

The countess made a haughty sound and then turned to leave. Or so Beau thought. After a few steps, she whirled back around.

"Who is Giorgio Amato?" she demanded.

"The MP from Cana. His wife is Amelie. She is from France. They have two children. Girls. Would you like their names?"

The Countess got *very* pinched-looking. "And who will be seated at the secondary table?"

"The parliamentary aides, and their guests. Twelve of each. I can recite names, if you'd like."

"That won't be necessary."

"Excellent." Then, to try to smooth things over, which was so foreign to her and yet necessary in this role as a *visible, respectable* princess, she continued. "I understand it must be…concerning to worry that I am not up to the challenge of taking on your role of hostess that you've held for the past year of Lyon's reign. Everyone has told me you were excellent at the job and made certain I knew I had incredibly big shoes to fill."

It was a bit of an exaggeration—another thing she wouldn't have done for herself. But for Lyon? She was an utter fool.

"You see, Countess, I have an excellent memory. It usually only takes reading something for it to be lodged here." Beau pointed to her temple. "Along with reading dossiers on every guest invited to the dinner, I have also read a book on Divio history, parliamentary etiquette, and the guide sent to guests. Is there anything else I should read?" Bend, bend, bend.

Just like her mother.

"Perhaps you should have asked me for help prior to the day before," the countess said.

Agree. Agree.

But her temper was snapping, and it felt *good*. Felt wonderful to feel something other a numb detachment from everything around her. "I'll ask Lyon for help if I need it." Then because that was *rude,* she tacked on a "thank you."

"He has a kingdom to run. Don't you think you've been distracting enough?"

Beau laughed. "Distracting?" Her husband barely looked at her, did everything he could to keep his physical distance. And sure, she'd leaned into that over the past few days, because she couldn't *bear* the thought of talking about schedules or when she had the best chance of getting pregnant.

But Beau doubted very much, no matter how happy Lyon claimed she made him, that she was any kind of *distraction*. Because he didn't want that, so she hadn't been that.

"He hasn't been the same since you came back from

that little honeymoon," the countess continued. "The fault of that lays directly in your lap."

Her lap? If only the fault of anything was hers, then maybe she could fix it. "Did it ever occur to you that the fault might be yours?" Beau countered. In the back of her mind she knew she was making a mistake. Lyon would be displeased.

And she just didn't *care* anymore. She wanted to break something. If it was them, so be it. "That it was you who put unreasonable expectations upon him? That you demanded he be so perfect that he's terrified of any misstep?" Beau did slam the book down then. She got to her feet and looked the shocked countess right in the eyes. "Or not you. Your mother, perhaps."

"How dare you speak of my mother."

"I have heard so much about her. In these bright, glowing terms, and yet all I see is a woman desperate for control, with no worry of how all that control might hurt and twist a little boy."

The countess reared back like she'd been slapped, and Beau knew she would pay for this. In so many ways this very moment would backfire on her, but she couldn't stop herself.

After all these weeks of shutting all her emotions away, she wanted to feel *everything*.

"I happen to think that perhaps *distraction* would be the best damn thing for a man who thinks the entire country's fate rests on every single step he takes."

Anger was power, but it was also emotion. And she felt it take over. The way her legs started to feel a little numb. Her vision started tunneling and for a terrifying moment she couldn't catch her breath.

She would not have a panic attack here in front of the countess. So she acted quickly. She walked right past her mother-in-law, ignoring the woman's sputtering protests. She didn't *run* to her rooms, but she hurried. Up the stairs. Trying to keep count in her head. Trying to breathe.

She reached the hallway to their rooms and nearly sobbed when Lyon stepped out of the door and into the hallway.

Not yet. Not yet. Not yet.

He said something, but she didn't hear it. She walked past him, not making any eye contact.

"Beau. What is the matter?"

She could hear him follow her, but she did not look back, she did not stop walking. But she forced herself to speak, as clearly as she could manage.

"I h-had a p-public fight with your mother. She said I've d-distracted you, so I told her I thought she had p-put unreasonable expectations on you and that is why you are s-so afraid of making a mistake that n-nothing else matters." The tears were starting, a sob threatening to escape, so she moved into the bedroom, and slammed the door behind her.

She locked the door as she sank to the floor, as the shakes took over. It felt like that moment back at Cristhian's house weeks ago, after listening to her father berate her for all her failures.

Because he had been right.

The only thing she could do was fail.

Lyon stared at the slammed door for countless seconds trying to make sense of what had just happened. He had never seen Beau even remotely that worked up. She'd been stuttering. Struggling to breathe. It almost reminded him of...

Then he heard footsteps and turned to see his mother charging into his sitting room where he stood. But it wouldn't do to talk here. If there'd already been a public fight, everything needed to be nipped in the bud *now*.

He stopped her then took her by the arm and led her across the hall into a little-used office.

He closed the door behind him, then surveyed his mother. Her color was high, her eyes were flashing with anger. For a moment, he was reminded of his grand-mother. A woman who he'd idolized.

I told her I thought she had put unreasonable expec-tations on you and that is why you are so afraid of mak-ing a mistake that nothing else matters.

Unreasonable wasn't fair. They'd placed expectations upon him because no one else could be trusted. No one else had been able to handle it. They had given him strength and belief in himself by thinking he could.

For a strange moment, he remembered that moment at the chalet. When Beau had apologized to him. A real apology. The kind his grandmother had claimed didn't exist. It had been the first time he'd ever considered the woman he'd idolized might be wrong.

But even before that, Beau hadn't understood him being a payment for a debt. No matter how he'd explained it, she hadn't been able to absorb it.

Because she simply didn't understand. Not because it was wrong... Right?

Any more it seemed like a cascade of wrong was hap-pening all around him.

"What has happened?" he asked. He had to focus on the task at hand. The public fight his mother and wife had just engaged in, and how he would...fix it.

"Your wife just made a scene, Lyon. First, she tried to show me up. Then she made wild accusations. And *then* she stormed away. This is why she was the hidden Rendall. She is a spoiled—"

"You will not speak of Beau in such a way to me," he said firmly.

"Did you *hear* me?" his mother all but screeched.

Lyon took his time responding to her. A wall of calm to his mother's upset. "You two had a little spat. Unfortunate."

Mother's eyes were wild, but she didn't yell anymore. She sucked in a careful breath. Venom throbbed in every word she spoke, but she spoke calmly and quietly. Mother and Grandmother had always done that so well. Tied up all their fury into cold, calm, *sharp* ice.

"In public, Lyon. Where any staff member could see. That she is *not* what you or this country needs."

He realized then his mistake—because the mistakes were always his. He was the one who would save everyone. From the moment he could remember, he'd known he was the payment of a debt. So all missteps were his. All messes his to clean up.

And he was failing. Over and over again.

He had assumed his mother would realize over time Beau was the perfect wife for him.

He should have made it more clear. So this fight was his fault. And he had to fix it. First, by showing his mother how ridiculous she was being. "Would you have me divorce her?" he asked blandly.

"Of course not. What a scandal! The *opposite* of the stability you *assured* me you could handle."

Lyon studied her then. Had he assured his mother of that? He couldn't remember anything but his grandmother and mother *insisting* that he handle it. Capable or not. It had always been up to *him*.

Now she was claiming he'd…taken that on himself?

"Then what would you have me do? What is it you think you are accomplishing with this attack on her? She is the princess. She is my wife. A wife you encouraged me to have. I cannot divorce her. So why are *you* adding to this scene?"

The outrage was written all over his mother's face, but it soon morphed into a sharp look that, again, reminded him of his grandmother. He braced himself for the attack, the takedown.

Because it always came after that look. From either woman.

"Perhaps this could be handled if you didn't have such a soft spot for her," Mother said in a viciously quiet voice. "*You* will make a mistake."

Yes, of course. *Him*.

He loosened his tie, that familiar choking feeling that was getting a little too common again. It seemed every day, no matter how careful he was, no matter all the precautions he took, those old anxious habits were creeping back in.

"You mustn't," his mother whispered at him. She leaned close, even though they were alone in this room with the door closed. She put her hand over his that was loosening his tie. "Have you been taking your medication?" She tried to tighten his tie for him, but he stepped back.

"Yes, Mother." A careful secret, of course, but the anxiety medication was the only way he'd gotten through his teenage years. Things had eased in his early twenties. After his grandmother's death…

Had he really never put it together before? He wanted to laugh. He'd told himself grief had eased the anxiety. One feeling taking over the other, but in retrospect that was ridiculous.

His anxiety had eased because one of the sources of it had been gone.

He shook his head. That was a terrible thought. A terrible way to feel about the woman who'd given him so much. Besides, this was all…the past. He needed to deal with the present. The parliamentary dinner was tomorrow, and everyone needed to be in accord. Everyone needed to be ready so they could continue to prove they were a strong, stable unit.

"What is it that bothers you about her?" Lyon asked. "Her as a person, or the soft spot you claim I have for her?"

"Claim? I have *eyes*. You are my son. I *know* you. The point of a wife was a partnership. An arrangement. Not…love."

Yes, that was true. That had been the point. And he'd never questioned it. Until something that felt far too close to *love* had taken hold. And he was afraid of soft spots, of desire, of losing his focus.

Of love.

Because he had been made to be afraid of all these things. But he also knew, that for all the ways he didn't remember his father, his mother had never once talked about him like a…pawn. He had not been an arrangement.

"You loved my father."

Mother blinked up at him, then turned away. "We must deal with the problem at hand. Not ancient history."

"Mother. You loved him."

As if sensing he wouldn't give up the topic, she sighed. "Yes." She turned away, refusing to look him in the eye. "What does that have to do with anything? I was not in charge, and never would be."

"Why would it be so terrible for me to love Beaugonia? Simply because I'm in charge?"

She turned back to face him, and he saw all the ways she looked like her own mother. The dark eyes, the way her mouth nearly disappeared when she was angry. "You are the ruler. You must love your country above all else. How else will you rise above the legacy the men in this family leave?"

Years ago, when he'd been quite young, he'd had the nerve to ask his grandmother why that responsibility had to fall to *him*. Why he was the only one.

She had slapped him across the face. He had cried. Which had earned him a night in his room without dinner. He hadn't thought of that in years. He'd blocked it out of his mind.

Lyon didn't care for old, ugly memories. He preferred to think of her as a strong leader. The woman who'd shaped him. But if she'd shaped Lyon… "Did she never give you a choice either?"

"What are you talking about?"

"What pressure did she put on you?"

"Who?"

"Your mother."

"Your grandmother…" Mother's brow furrowed and she shook her head. "This is ridiculous. Your wife created a scene and now you want to discuss your grandmother with me?"

"Yes. Because it all goes back to her, doesn't it? Why we're here. Worried about…scenes. Afraid of love and soft spots. Things that normal people think are *good*."

"That poor woman watched her family destroy every tradition, every positive relationship, every bit of honor her father and grandfather had built. And instead of letting it destroy her, she focused on us. How we could save it. It could never be me, Lyon. That's hardly her fault or some pressure she put upon me. But she taught me just the same, for when I would give her a son."

A payment to a debt. He'd always accepted that as a perfectly acceptable thing to put on a child. But there was something about soft spots, and the possibility of love. The idea of making his own child with Beaugonia, and the way she'd looked at him when he'd tried to explain. It all added up into a sick feeling in his stomach.

His child would never be a payment to anything. They would be a *person*. An heir, yes, but a *child* first.

"Give *her* a son?" he asked his mother gently.

She whirled away, frustration and temper in every harsh move. "You sound so much like your father right now. And he was *wrong* about her. He *died*, and she and you remained."

"Wrong about her? I thought Grandmother approved of him?"

"*She* did. Because he was a good man from a good family. Upstanding and honest. Your father found your grandmother…difficult. But he simply didn't understand. He wasn't royal."

This was the first Lyon had ever heard of it. The first he'd ever asked. Because…his grandmother had discouraged any talk of those already gone. Or so she said, though she spoke of her own father plenty. "Did you think he didn't understand. Or did Grandmother think that?"

Mother looked up at him like he'd just stabbed her clean through. "Why are we talking about this, Lyon?"

He didn't know. Only that it was crystallizing things for him. Things he'd been trying to push away ever since the chalet. All the ways Beau had, without meaning to, flipped the truths he'd believed from his grandmother on their head.

And he looked at his mother now and saw himself. She had believed his grandmother's hard, cold truths. But someone had loved her, and she had loved someone. Father had been her soft spot, and then he'd died. Too soon, too young.

"Losing him must have been very hard."

"People die," she said, but he heard the grief in her voice all the same.

"Yes, that was Grandmother's line, wasn't it?"

Mother straightened, lifted her chin. "She was right. Everyone must deal with death. There is no point in grieving, in letting it mark you."

"I don't think all emotions have to have a point, Mother. They're just there." Anxiety. Grief.

Love.

Such a false equivalency they'd passed down. That one love might blot out another. That responsibility to his wife would mean disaster for his country.

But wasn't that the false equivalency he'd employed back at the chalet? Desire would lead to forgoing all... sense, responsibility.

"Have you ever wondered, Madre?" he said gently. "If Grandmother put an unreasonable weight upon our shoulders?"

"She only wanted what was best for Divio. And you should as well. Letting that wife of yours *poison* you is beneath you."

But he saw something desperate in his mother's eyes. Like he had gotten at least a little through to her, even if she wouldn't admit it.

"I do want what's best for Divio. And I will fight for it. But why does that mean I cannot care for my own wife?"

"She's poisoned you."

"Or she's set me free." He wasn't certain he believed that, but it felt good to say. It felt *true* to say. "Now, I would appreciate it if you would have lunch with Beau. I will go talk to her, and then you two will sit down and have a civil conversation. A *public* civil conversation to undo this."

Mother scoffed. "She will not agree. Or she will not be civil. You cannot get through to that girl. She is... *unhinged*."

"She is not. She's incredibly reasonable. But she's also...incredibly herself. Without fear. Nevertheless, she will have lunch with you, she will be civil, because I'll have asked her to. You see, Mother… Perhaps I have a soft spot for her, but she has a soft spot for me as well. Grandmother treated us like little soldiers. There were no soft spots. I thought that was the only way to be."

"It got you here, didn't it?"

"No, happenstance did. Maybe the other family's genetic predispositions to giving in to excess as well, I can't deny that. Perhaps Grandmother taught me in ways her brothers, nephews and so on had never been taught. Perhaps it will even allow me to rule Divio with all that tradition and stability she so worshipped. But it didn't *get me* here."

"She loved you."

Lyon thought about that. And then he thought about Beau. How she listened to him. Tried to understand him. The comfort she offered. The heartfelt apology. Those things were closer to love than cold demands, hard rules and harsh punishments.

"No. I'm not sure she really loved either of us. She loved the idea of what her progeny might do to one-up her brothers. Love is…helping one another, apologizing when you're wrong. Love is soft spots, Mother."

"You must run a country, Lyon."

"Yes. I've been doing an excellent job of it the past year, if I do say so myself. It was good, to start off just me. But now I have added a wife, and some adjustments could be made. If I am going to start a family, adjustments *will* be made." He would not raise his children with the weight of the entire country on their shoulders.

Respect for their role, yes. An appreciation for hard

work, ideally. But he would not lay down the burden of centuries. Not on them. Not on his wife.

And not even on himself. Not anymore.

CHAPTER FOURTEEN

LYON RETURNED TO their rooms. The door to the bedroom was still closed, and when he went to try and open it, he found it locked.

He knocked. "Beau?" he called through the door. "You must unlock the door for me. We need to talk." He would confess everything. Love and soft spots and what he hoped for the future. He would tell her the realizations she'd brought out.

And together, they would build some sort of future where his fear of failure did not rule him. Where he could make *her* as happy as she'd made him.

But she didn't respond in any way. And the door did not unlock. He jiggled the knob once more. "Beau?" He set his ear to the door. It wasn't like she could have disappeared. She had to be in there somewhere. Perhaps she'd gone into the bathroom and couldn't hear.

He had a key to this door somewhere, but he didn't want to have to call Mr. Filini to track it down as then there'd be speculation as to why his wife had locked him out of their bedroom. Or should that matter? Should he—

Then he heard it. Not her responding, but the faint sounds of…gasping? Like she was struggling to breathe. She must be having some kind of…medical event.

Terror speared through him, and he shook the door in renewed earnest. "Beau? Answer me."

He didn't hear her say anything, but as he was rearing back to fling himself against the door, the knob moved. Then the door creaked open the tiniest crack.

He rushed forward into the room, heart pounding and worry and fear clawing through him. The light was dim—the curtains drawn. He looked around in a panic, and didn't see her at first, but he heard her. A terrible, gasping noise. Coming from...

She was on the floor. Tears were pouring out of her eyes, and every breath sounded labored and terrible. She shook like she might simply shake apart.

For only a second he was rendered completely frozen with terror. "I'll get the doctor," he managed to say. He wanted to run to her, but she needed help he couldn't give.

She shook her head violently. She opened her mouth but no sound came out. Then he strode forward, gathered her in his arms. "I will *take* you to the doctor," he said firmly.

"It's n-not an ill—illness," she managed to say, though her voice was weak and her entire being shook in his arms.

"Then what—?" But the fact she could speak now had eased something inside of him enough to recognize certain things. If it wasn't medical, that meant it was something else. And the only something else that he knew could have physical symptoms like that was anxiety.

"You've had a panic attack," he murmured in surprise. It was hard to believe Beau panicked about *anything*.

She didn't respond, but she leaned into him and he

held on. He settled them both onto the bed, her in his lap as he rocked her gently and murmured reassuring words that she was all right. She would be all right.

It took time. First, she began to breathe easier. Then the tears stopped and she allowed him to brush the wet off her face. The shakes remained, but they lessened in severity. When he thought she was calm enough to talk, he ran a hand over her hair and held her close.

"Is this because of the fight with my mother? I've handled it, *tesoruccia*." He pressed a kiss to her temple. Something inside of him that had been tied tight these weeks eased.

This was right. Not that she would be in such a state, but that they would be close. That he would hold her and she would lean against him. That they would have soft spots for one another. That they would *talk*.

Not hide from everything they were. And poor Beaugonia had gotten herself into such a frenzy she'd had a panic attack. Which was probably his own fault. He'd put too many responsibilities on *her* shoulders.

Well, no more.

"We must talk, Beau. We must… This has not been working, has it? I am to blame. We will sort it all out. Don't worry any more, *amore mio*. Everything will be fine."

But she shook her head, even as she sagged against him. "It will never be fine."

"Beaugonia…"

"These attacks are never because of one thing," she said, sounding utterly exhausted. "I admit, this one stemmed from my argument with your mother, but that's hardly the reason I have panic attacks."

Anything that eased began to tighten up again. Those words... *These*...attacks...as if a panic attack was a common occurrence for her. Not because of something he'd done. Not because of a pressure that was too much.

He looked down at her tousled hair. He tried to make sense of this. She'd mentioned her childhood social anxiety, and he'd understood. His anxiety had not been related to crowds. It had been more...generalized. But he'd never had a full-blown panic attack. Or at least, nothing that looked like this. Still, he could see how if it had been left unchecked, he might have.

But she had claimed that...she had grown out of her anxiety. That it no longer defined her, though her parents had continued to define her by it. He had assumed that perhaps, like him, she had gotten help. Because she *had* been fine in all social situations. She had been perfect at their wedding dinner, on the video. She handled the staff well, and her position.

Maybe she had gotten help but because they hadn't communicated, such help had fallen by the wayside. Maybe this was just... He didn't know. He was misunderstanding something, surely. "Do you take anything?"

"Take anything?" she repeated, like she didn't understand the question.

"Medication? For anxiety or panic disorders?"

"I..." She shook her head. "No. My father was insistent I never be treated. I did research on my own, but I was too...worried about what might happen if he caught me with medication or speaking to a therapist even via video. It was a blight against our name, in his eyes."

"Your father..." And then a few facts started to fall into place. The fact this was not...new, or out of place.

Her father and research and the resigned way she spoke of all this, like she knew exactly how this went.

She didn't have medication because it was not allowed.

Because *this* was commonplace. And had been.

And she had never told him.

"How often do you have these attacks?" he asked, still searching for some way to understand this that did not cause this terrible rending inside of him.

She stiffened against him, then began to ease away. He would have held on to her, but his limbs felt numb.

"I'm feeling much better. Do you mind if I take a bath? And then a nap? I'm quite tired." She didn't get to her feet, but she edged away so there was space between them on the end of the bed.

He could only stare at her. Avoiding the question. A simple question. What should be *simple*. Unless she'd been lying to him. "Beau."

She sighed heavily. "Yes, I have panic attacks. They are sporadic. Uncontrollable. Sometimes there is a cause, sometimes there is not. You needn't worry about it."

He made a noise. He wasn't sure what kind of noise, but no words would encompass his reaction to *You needn't worry about it*. He *was* worried. She'd *terrified* him.

She'd *lied* to him. To his face. Over and over again for all these weeks.

"I *can* hide it," she said firmly. "I have been hiding it. And still, you're the only one who knows beyond my family. It's all right. No one else has to know. You needn't…" She trailed off, but she didn't look at him.

He was still sitting on the bed, trying to work through this turn of events. "What is it you think I'll do?"

A long looming silence settled in between them. She didn't answer, kept her gaze on the opposite wall, and he found himself relieved.

He didn't want to know what horrible thing she thought of him, it turned out.

All this time, and she'd been lying to him. Hiding this from him. And then it dawned on him. Not just this lie, but… "This is why your father did not want you to be his heir."

For a moment she did not respond. He heard her swallow. "Yes."

This was the secret his mother had been worried she'd been keeping. It was hardly the end of any worlds. If she'd kept it a secret this long in her life, they could continue to do so. It wasn't the panic attacks themselves, he of all people understood that one could not always control the things the brain did.

But she had *lied* to him. She did not trust him with this information even now. When he'd been ready to…

Change *everything* for her. Admit soft spots and *love*, and this was how little she thought of him. He knew she hadn't been happy, but he thought she felt at least some of what he did.

Surely there was just something he wasn't understanding. He needed more information. "How many have you had since coming here?"

She looked over at him miserably. "Does it matter?"

That she had had them? Hid them? Lied to him? And still he thought details would somehow…help ease this yawning ache inside of him growing deeper and more painful by the moment. "How many?"

She looked down at her lap. "Three."

Three. They had been married only three weeks. She had hidden *three* panic attacks from him. Well, two. But she would have hidden this from him if he hadn't... "When were they?"

"I'm very tired and—"

"When were they, Beaugonia?"

She lifted her chin. There was something, a hint of *life* in her eyes, but it was shrouded in a misery that settled in him like a stab to the gut.

"If you must know, though it matters not at all. The first night at the chalet. Last week in the library. Today, after arguing with your mother."

The chalet. "How... But we were in such close quarters at the chalet. How?"

"I know how to hide it. I told you. It was the middle of the night. I got out of bed without waking you."

And then she'd come back. Lied to him about being cold. And then... Lyon got to his feet. He wanted to rip the collar off his neck, the pressure squeezing just there. He stalked away from her, then turned back.

"So once a week. Once a week you've had these... attacks. And hidden it from me?"

"Yes." She didn't sound the least bit repentant. She just sat there on the bed, staring at her lap.

"Why would you have kept this from me?"

Her head whipped up. "Are you joking? A weakness like this? When you're obsessed with being seen as stable and respectable? Why would I ever admit this to you?"

"Obsessed." It felt like an indictment. One he could hardly defend himself from. It was true.

Except he hardly viewed a panic attack as some *weakness*. The fact she thought he would…

"Can you please leave me be now? I'd like to rest. Alone."

Alone. When he'd thought… It was all too much. He needed to sort through the…layers of it all. So perhaps alone would be best. She could rest and he could think.

But he didn't want anything hanging over her head, worrying her unnecessarily. "You do not need to attend the parliamentary dinner if you do not wish." He would make her excuses. Find a way to make certain she didn't have to deal with it. "I'll leave the decision up to you."

She looked at him then, her hazel eyes reflecting a hurt he did not understand. She didn't say anything.

So he gave her what she wanted. Time to rest. *Alone.*

Beau didn't rest. Because she felt the wreckage of everything like a sharp weight against her lungs.

He would never look at her the same. He would hide her away.

You do not need to attend the parliamentary dinner if you do not wish.

He did not need to be any clearer. He was embarrassed by her now. She'd ruined everything. All the years of refusing to believe what her parents thought of her, but now…

Maybe they were right. She was weak. And Lyon needed strength, stability, respectability. That could never be her.

What is it you think I'll do?

He'd sounded so horrified. So affronted.

Lock me away. Hate me.

She wouldn't stand for it. Not again. Maybe she loved him. Maybe it broke her heart into a million pieces, but she would not be locked away. And if she told herself it was *that*, and not that the worst thing she could imagine was having to live with him knowing he viewed her as what she was: *less*, then maybe she could get through this.

Because there were always options. She could fall apart. She could let this break her into all the pieces she stitched together after each and every panic attack. Or she could refuse to be ended no matter how much her heart hurt.

She hadn't been herself for weeks now. So maybe this was an opportunity. To get back to the person she'd been before she'd been stupid enough to soften her heart to someone who expected perfection.

That Beau had been strong, determined, sure of herself. Maybe there'd been a decided lack of joy, a loneliness, particularly after Zia had run away and she'd been left alone with her parents, but she hadn't felt destroyed.

Nothing was worse than this feeling. It would choke her until there was nothing left. She had to…get out.

She grabbed her phone, called Zia. "Zia. I know you're busy, and the babies must come first, but…"

"Beau, what is it?"

"I need help. I need…to run away." It was the only answer. She wouldn't be locked away. She wouldn't be hidden. She wouldn't keep living this…strange, gray version of turning into her mother.

She wouldn't stay and make Lyon unhappy. He would be angry about that, because it didn't look good from the outside, but she was tired of the damn outside. He could make up a lie. The version of her that was his wife could be a story people told, just like the story of her as a princess had always been.

She existed. She wasn't seen. Only instead of hiding in his castle, she would be free. She would be *free*.

Zia had run away and all had worked out, so this would too.

"What's happened? Did he hurt you? I'll kill him. Well, no, I'll send Cristhian to kill him. That's far scarier."

She wanted to be warmed by the viciousness in Zia's voice, but she didn't feel the least bit bloodthirsty. She wasn't *angry* at Lyon. She was just…devastated. "No, no. It isn't that."

"Then what is it?"

"Lyon…discovered my panic attacks."

There was a beat of silence. "Did you think you could hide it forever?" Zia asked gently.

The truth was, Beau had thought exactly that. Or maybe held on to the hope she was in control of some facet of her life and that she would be able to.

All up in smoke now.

"No, I suppose not, but… I can't be what Lyon needs me to be now. He knows I'm defective, and he'll hide me away."

"Did he call you that?" Zia demanded. "I *am* going to kill him. With my bare hands."

Beau thought back. No, he hadn't said anything like her father would have, but she'd seen it in his face. In the way he'd pulled back. He saw her differently now. Maybe there was enough kindness in him not to say it to her face, but she was broken now in his eyes.

She would not make him happy now that he knew this. She could not be the partner he needed, expected. "Not in so many words, no. He has a kindness to him. This isn't about…cruelty. I just can't be someone's dirty little secret again, hidden away. I won't be."

Again, Zia was silent for a few seconds. "All right. Then we'll get you out. All you have to do is get out of the palace. Find somewhere to hide. No need to call. Cristhian will find you. It's what he does."

"But the babies…"

"I am hardly alone, Beau. I have help. Cristhian will find you. And we'll have you back here before the day is out. Here and safe. I promise. Just get out of the palace."

Beau looked around the room that had begun to feel like hers. The life that held both misery and joy. Complicated feelings she'd never expected. A life she wanted… and couldn't have.

At least that was familiar.

Then she hung up the phone.

And planned her escape.

CHAPTER FIFTEEN

LYON HAD A staff member tell his mother there'd be no lunch. Then he had meetings to attend. He brooded, the whole afternoon, trying to determine what the hell to do with all this.

And he approved all the last-minute changes and hiccups on the parliamentary dinner. He dealt with problems, questions. He was distracted, *yes*, but he was not incapable of doing what needed to be done because of it.

Because, it turned out, the women who'd raised him were wrong. He could do both. Love and grieve and hurt and make good choices for his country. It turned *out*, that when he gave himself a chance to do everything without the fear of taking a wrong step, he did what he'd always done.

The right damn thing. Soft spots or no.

Perhaps a time would come when that would not be the case, but even if he held himself to some impossible standard of isolation—upsets would still come along. Natural disasters or worldly problems challenging all Divio was. Loss or illness or who knew what else when it came to his family, to himself.

He could do the right thing—avoid scandal, meet

his responsibilities—but he could not control the world around him by doing such things.

It was a strange, out-of-body moment, all in all. To be both distracted and capable of dealing with—or delegating—everything that needed to be done. To watch as nothing crumbled around him simply because his role wasn't the only thing he took into account.

To consider that maybe, just maybe, there could be a life where he balanced both. Not the expectations his grandmother had set for him, but meeting the needs of his citizens. While at the same time meeting the needs of his family, without letting selfish desires ruin everything. Without worrying that…every private decision would ruin his public persona.

Beau was his family. His wife. He hated the idea that she suffered so. It tore him up inside and made him want to go talk to her and beg forgiveness. He would protect her and defend her from *anyone* who dared say a negative word about her.

But she had *lied*. She had kept this from him from the very beginning. She had been in the wrong as well. Whether it was his fault or not that she hadn't trusted him with this, had hidden it from him, she had not given him the opportunity to be right or wrong.

They both needed to find a way to do that. Give each other chances, instead of being too afraid and making everything worse. Making everything get to the point of falling apart.

Maybe balance wasn't so much about everyone being one hundred percent happy or everything getting his full attention. No, it was finding what needed him the most in the moment and responding to it.

Because his grandmother's will to one-up her brother had no bearing anymore. Both were dead and gone. He was here. Beau was here.

Right now, everything was set for the dinner tomorrow, he'd responded to every pressing item on his agenda. So what needed him was Beau, and working through what had happened today.

If he owed her an apology, which he did, he should offer it. And if she did not offer one of her own, then he would deal with that in the moment. They would talk through it. Have those conversations that had been sorely missing in her book until the very end.

But when those conversations had come—the couple in the book had worked things out. So that is what he would do. Make it all work out.

He left his office and went in search of her. It was late, but she wasn't in their suite of rooms or in bed, so he went to the library next. And when she wasn't there, he began to...worry. He searched everywhere he could think of, and then finally he had to page her assistant.

The woman was wide-eyed and nervy when she came into his office. She had clearly been asleep. Her curtsey was awkward at best. "I'm sorry, Your Highness, it seems no one has seen her since this morning."

"This *morning*." Lyon's body felt as though it emptied fully out, then inch by inch filled back with rage.

All the ways she'd pushed him. All the ways she'd claimed to want him. All the ways she had understood him, and she hadn't given him the damn opportunity to understand *her*.

She had run away.

Where—but Lyon immediately knew where she would

have gone. The only place she would run away to. She talked to her sister almost every day. The only thing she ever spoke of with any positivity was Zia and her babies.

"Find out the residence of Zia Rendall…or whatever her name is now. And ready a plane. Once you have the address, I will leave at once."

"I… I don't know…"

He growled, couldn't help himself. Luckily Mr. Filini entered, unfortunately his mother did as well. Someone must have woken her up and told her Beau was missing. Oh, well. It didn't matter. All that mattered was getting to Beau.

"Mr. Filini—"

"I heard, Your Highness. We'll be on it at once." He gestured to Beau's assistant and they both left.

Lyon thought briefly of packing, but what did he need? Nothing. He would bring her back here and they would have their reckoning. She did not get to just *run away* and have that be that.

"Lyon, you can't miss the dinner," Mother said.

He looked at his mother. For a moment there was a pang. She was right. He should stay. Focus on responsibilities first and *then* deal with Beau. He couldn't possibly risk the potential he might not get back in time. What would people say?

It was knee-jerk. Everything he'd been taught. *What would people say?* They would compare him to all the negative that had come before.

But if he gave it space. If he let himself consider it for what it was, not the debt he had to pay, it became ridiculous.

Responsibility to host some frivolous, meaningless

dinner? That had nothing to do with the actual rules of law or running of the kingdom. That wasn't in service to the citizens but was simply meant to feed a bunch of pompous members of parliament, so they decided to *like* him? And maybe, just *maybe*, not compare him to the reckless men who'd preceded him?

To hell with that.

"If I am not back in time, I trust you can handle it."

She sputtered, but he didn't bother to listen to any responses she managed.

He was going to find his wife.

Cristhian had indeed found her. That was what he did, after all. And in no time at all Beau had been on a plane, flying back to his estate with him. He didn't offer her any words, didn't try to get her to talk. He simply ushered her where she needed to go. He was a good man. Worthy of Zia and their beautiful twins.

Who Beau would finally get to hold.

When she arrived at Cristhian and Zia's that afternoon, she was greeted by her sister, who had one baby in the crook of her arm, and the other arm open and ready for Beau.

Beau was not much of a crier. She had always chalked it up to crying so much when she had panic attacks. It took away any need to release her emotions that way when she wasn't panicking.

But when she stepped into Zia's outstretched arm, and Zia hugged her close, the tears filled her eyes. She blinked them away before she pulled back and looked at the tiny bundle in Zia's arms.

"This is Harrison," Zia said, her voice rough. A mewling cry, followed by a much angrier one, sounded from deeper in the house. "And there is your namesake announcing her displeasure, as she is quite adept at doing. Come." Zia led her into the house and a cozy little living room with all sorts of baby paraphernalia strewn about, including two little bassinets in the corner.

Beau followed Zia to one and looked down at an angry little bundle. Her face was red and scrunched up.

"And this is Begonia. Our little Bee," Zia said, the love and joy in every word even as the girl screamed in a tiny but loud cry. "Go on," Zia said, nudging Beau with her hip. "Pick her up."

But Beau felt completely ill-equipped to deal with any of this. Or any of her life right now. It was all too big and unwieldy. She swallowed the emotion clogging her throat, or tried. "I don't know how."

"Allow me." Cristhian scooped the baby up, and the girl immediately began to quiet.

Something about a very large man holding a very small bundle made Beau want to weep. But she held it together and Zia moved her over to the couch, and then Cristhian sat next to Beau. Beau tried to hold her arms like Zia was and Cristhian transferred baby Bee into Beau's arms. Zia sat next to her, cradling Harrison.

It was just so amazing and beautiful. That her sister had brought these two precious lives into the world. Beau gazed down at the little girl in her lap. "Aren't they the most perfect things in the entire universe?"

"Mostly. I don't *quite* have those feelings when they're screaming their heads off at two in the morning, but ninety-nine percent of the time they are the most perfect things in the entire universe." Zia stroked her son's cheek.

After a few minutes of silence, Zia sighed. "What's happened, Beau?"

Beau couldn't tear her gaze away from Bee. She couldn't really find the words either. "I don't know. It was so good at first, and then…"

"Good?" Zia pressed. "You…got along with Lyon?"

Beau nodded. "I wasn't lying to you during all those calls. I…" *Love him.* "He was very kind. He has the most beautiful library, and he likes to read. He even read a book I liked to get to know me. It was actually… I was very happy for a bit. Maybe if I'd been pregnant, it would have gone differently."

Which was not a productive thought. She'd just be sitting in his castle being miserable. Not allowed to go to things like parliamentary dinners. Even though she'd proven she could handle it. A baby wouldn't have changed anything, except she would have had someone to hold in her isolation.

"So you two… You…" Zia cleared her throat. "There was…a *chance* you were…pregnant?"

Beau looked up at her sister, then realized Zia had clearly not considered that just because the marriage had been arranged to save Zia, that there might not be the making of heirs involved.

"We had sex, Zia. We *are* married."

Cristhian made a dismayed sort of noise and stood. "Perhaps I will go…do *anything* else."

Zia rolled her eyes and waved him off. "We can handle the babies. Go do something manly."

He smiled at Zia, the kind of smile that spoke of many things. Affection, amusement, intimacy. Zia watched her husband leave, the love so evident in her eyes that Beau had to look away. But she could only look at the child in her lap and feel a terrible, terrible yearning.

"I wanted to be pregnant," she heard herself say, without really meaning to.

"Oh, Beau." Zia's free arm came around Beau's shoulders.

She shook her head. It was the wrong thing to say. She blinked back the tears. "Best this way."

"Tell me what happened. All of it. Beginning to end, and then we will figure out what to do."

Beau didn't really want to rehash it yet, but she might as well. She didn't know where to start, really. At the wedding? The chalet? Even though she spoke to Zia almost every day, she had mostly kept her sister in the dark about the Lyon Beau had come to know. She hadn't known how to talk about falling in love with the man she'd married to save Zia. She hadn't known how to talk about sex, because it hadn't felt right to talk about Lyon's reaction to things. And maybe she didn't want Zia flying into protective mode when Zia had been carrying so much on her plate. So Beau had been vague about everything.

Now? She told her sister everything. From Lyon's "steps" to the chalet to the horrible fight with the countess. To Lyon discovering her. In the midst of a panic attack.

"This dinner has been everyone's focus for weeks," Beau said. She'd managed to hold back tears, but it was getting harder. "Talked about how important it is for the guests to see a united monarchy. To be fed and wooed and complimented as if that will wash away the poor deeds of the past princes. And maybe it would. Men in power are so very simple. But the moment Lyon saw me... The moment he realized what was happening... He saw what's wrong with me and then because of that he said I didn't have to go."

"He sounds like Father," Zia said with disgust.

Beau so wished she could agree. "But he's not. Not in the least." Maybe that's why she felt bruised straight through. Maybe that's why running away didn't feel right or righteous, just depressing.

She didn't want to punish Lyon, didn't want to hurt him. Which added to the depression. "If anything, I've fallen into being our mother."

"Impossible," Zia said, but it was knee-jerk, she didn't *know*.

"I pretzeled myself to make him happy. I... I made myself *miserable* to make him happy."

"That's not quite the same as Mother, Beau," Zia said gently.

Beau stared at Zia in utter shock. "How can you even try to claim that?"

"Mother...isn't miserable. I'm not saying she's happy, but she's not...trying to make Father *happy*."

"She certainly wasn't attempting to make us or herself happy."

"No. I think she's afraid of Father. Of what he'll do. How he'll react. She never stood up for us, not because she *loved* him more than us—though I admittedly thought that for a time. But... I'm in love now. Both with my husband, and I have these children whom I love. Mother is all...fear. All that talk of bending and not breaking. She just wants things to be easy and smooth. Love is neither of those things. For good or for ill. It takes...work, compromise. It means losing pieces of your heart to be out of your own control. It's why it was so easy for her to just…let us be married and then wash her hands of us. It's easier that way, than to maintain a relationship."

Beau frowned a little at that. She hadn't expected love to be easy. No book had ever claimed it would be such. So maybe it's why it never occurred to her that her mother's motivation was the path of least resistance, not some passionate love that only extended to her husband and not her children.

"There is a certain give-and-take to love." Zia looked at her children. "Perhaps it helps that I had them, growing inside of me, long before I considered *love*. If I'd only felt my love for Cristhian, perhaps it would have terrified me to turn into Mother too. But them? Oh, Beau. I'd give them anything. I'd give up anything to make them safe and healthy and happy. And that extends to my husband. So, I can't believe it's…wrong to want to make someone happy. There's something right about that. Something *loving* about that."

"So you think I should go back and be miserable and hide away and—"

Zia put her free hand on Beau's shoulder. "Not at all. I said give *and* take. Not you giving and him taking. If he thinks because of one little panic attack you're somehow not worthy of going to dinner, he can sod off forever. That's on *him*. Not you. And it's nothing at all to do with love."

Beau didn't understand why that didn't make her feel any better, but she pushed it all aside and focused on her sister. Her niece and nephew. On simple, easy love.

But was it *simple* when she'd sacrificed herself for

Zia? When Zia had sacrificed herself for Beau for years? Or was that give? And take. Hard decisions to make someone else happy. A willingness to survive the miserable, if someone else could be okay.

But Beau didn't want her life to be what it had always been, so how could she go back to Lyon? Since there was no easy answer to that, she ignored it. She had a nice afternoon with her sister. A reaffirming evening watching Cristhian and Zia act as a team. The love they shared with each other and their children was clear.

Beau couldn't go back to a life that didn't look like that, so she'd done the right thing.

Of course, she didn't know what to do about the future. Lyon would hardly grant a divorce. But, she couldn't go back. Maybe it was her turn to disappear. Zia had gone to a little polar island for a while when she'd first discovered her pregnancy, maybe Beau could follow suit.

She would be alone, but wasn't that better than hiding half of herself to please someone? Or being hidden away in a castle that wasn't hers? Better to isolate herself than be isolated by others. She had always thought so, and she tended to be right.

Late into the evening, really early morning at this point, she helped Zia with the twins' middle-of-the-night feeding. They sat together on the couch under a very dim light, Beau feeding Harrison with a bottle while Zia held Bee to her. Even in her fog of misery, this felt so nice. To be an adult with her sister. To sit here in a life that did not involve their parents or threats or *kingdoms*. Just late nights and quiet rooms and sweet babies.

Cristhian came in. He was dressed in dark sweats and a T-shirt, his hair sleep-rumpled.

Zia looked up at him with some surprise. "Beau helped me. You should have kept sleeping."

But Cristhian was giving Beau an odd look, before he turned to his wife. "Zia? Can I talk to you for a second?" He nodded toward the hallway.

A secret. Beau frowned. Zia raised an eyebrow.

"I'm in the middle of something, darling," she replied dryly, pointing to the child latched to her.

"Yes. I know. It's only…"

Beau shared a look with Zia, because never any time had she ever seen Cristhian seem even remotely uncertain as he did now.

And then she heard a shout from somewhere deeper in the house. Both Beau and Zia straightened with alarm.

"Is something wrong?" Zia asked.

Cristhian cleared his throat. "Well. It seems the prince has arrived."

"Who's the prince…?" Beau began to ask, but then it dawned on her. She recognized that shout, though she had never heard Lyon shout in such a way. Her eyes widened. What was he doing here? "Oh."

Oh.

Zia reached over, clutched her arm. "You don't have to see him if you don't want to. Cristhian will send him away."

"We have tried." Cristhian cleared his throat. "He is quite…insistent."

"So insist him right back," Zia said fiercely, as she transferred Bee to her shoulder and rubbed the baby's back until a small burp sounded. "With your fist," she added darkly, a very strange tableau.

But not as strange as Lyon being here. *Here.*

"I'm trying to avoid an international incident," Cristhian replied, his voice equally as dry as Zia's had been earlier.

"Well, I'm not." Zia got to her feet as if she was about to go instigate such incident. But before anyone could do anything, Lyon stormed right into the room.

His hair was wild, his tie loose and one of the top buttons of his shirt unbuttoned.

For ticking moments, Beau could only stare at him. He was as unkempt as she'd ever seen him. He was angry, certainly, and in *front* of people. And still her heart leapt.

What an idiot she was. What a stupid thing love was. She clutched Harrison close and steeled herself for whatever he was going to say.

Because she wouldn't go back and shrink herself. No matter what she'd done, no matter what she'd promised. She would be free.

And he could go to hell.

CHAPTER SIXTEEN

LYON WAS RUNNING on little sleep and too much anger. He had thought he would calm down by the time he arrived at Cristhian Sterling's estate from simple exhaustion if nothing else, but every minute of knowing Beau had run away, without *talking* to him, poked his temper higher.

When Cristhian's staff and then Cristhian himself had tried to bar Lyon from Beau, it had been the last straw. Whatever last dredges of propriety and concern for his image had gone up in smoke.

I will see my wife.

And he had been prepared to fight whoever might try to stop him. But once Cristhian had left, it had only taken moving past the sleepy man trying to tell him that he wasn't welcome.

Who gave a damn about *welcome*?

He had heard quiet voices and followed them down a hallway. He had charged into the room but came to a halting stop. He saw Beau right away. She sat on a cozy-looking couch, dressed in fuzzy pajamas. Her hair was pulled back. But it wasn't the gorgeous, perfect sight of her that stopped him dead.

She was holding the smallest infant he'd ever seen.

For a moment the sight took him so off guard, he had no words. He could only *stare*.

After a few moments like that, she stood. "You cannot simply barge into people's houses this late at night," she said to him, haughty and royal. She moved over to Cristhian and handed the baby off.

Then she turned to him, chin up, eyes flashing.

"And yet here I am," he returned, wanting her and wanting to *shake* her in equal measure. He pointed a finger at her. "And *you* are going to listen to me."

"You'll be careful where you point that finger," Zia said, stepping in between his finger and Beau.

He surveyed the sister he'd been meant to marry. She had once even worn his ring. It felt like a different lifetime ago, all that. Like he'd been a different person then. He supposed he had been.

And now she stood here, holding her own child, with her husband watching with wary eyes, and a child in his own arms.

"Ah, my former fiancée." Lyon gave a short, sarcastic bow. "So good to see you again now that we are in-laws."

Her eyes narrowed. "For now."

Over his dead body.

But he didn't care about Zia. He cared about his *wife*. Who stood in this dim room with anger and hurt flashing in her eyes, and no *shame*. When she *should* feel shame because she had *run away*.

"Perhaps we should give them their privacy," Cristhian murmured to his wife.

But Zia was staring at Lyon with daggers in her eyes. "Over my dead body."

"I don't care who stays or goes," Lyon muttered, mov-

ing around Zia so that Beau was in front of him instead.
Nothing mattered except this woman. So he stopped en-
gaging with the two other people in the room, and focused on why he was here.

On what needed to be said.

"You should not have run away, Beaugonia." He supposed there were better ways to say that, better ways to
start this. He supposed any of the speeches he'd practiced
on the flight here might have gone over better.

But it was all he could think. He loved this woman,
had somehow realized all the ridiculous things holding
him back on account of his childhood because of her,
and she had *run*.

"You should return to Divio at once," she replied.
"You are making a scene and it is nearly morning. If you
are not careful, you will miss your dinner."

"To hell with the dinner!" He shouted it. Really shouted
it. He could not remember the last time he'd actually allowed himself to *shout*.

It felt too damn good. *Slippery slope*. And maybe it
was. To allow himself to feel. To allow himself to run
with emotion and make a mistake because of it. Maybe
he was ruining everything.

But if he ruined it and she came back to him, it would
all be worth it.

She blinked at him. Finally, *finally* completely taken
aback. It lit something inside of him. One of those dangerous fires he wasn't supposed to indulge.

But what did it matter here? It was only him and her.

And her sister and brother-in-law, and two infants,
but they weren't even royalty any longer. And the babies
couldn't speak. So.

"I do not know why you are so angry, Lyon. But I am not going back. We… We are ill-suited. I know that will be a problem for you, but so would be staying. I'm sure we can reach some sort of private agreement to maintain a public image. But I can't—"

He couldn't let her say another word. "You don't know why I'm angry?" He had not thought he could be more incandescent with rage, and that she would be so…outrageously ridiculous. "I am angry at you lying to me. I am angry that you hid something so important from me. And I made a gesture out of *kindness* to allow you not to attend the dinner that I *wanted* you at, as my wife. As my partner. As…everything you are, and you *ran*. Without so much as a word."

"Kindness?" she all but shrieked. "A kindness? To want me not to attend your precious dinner because I'm such an embarrassment?"

"Embarrassment?" He yelled it right back. To hell with decorum and anything else. He was so angry he didn't even notice the two people holding babies quietly leave the room. "Who said anything of the kind? I *love* you. I would do anything for you. And instead of giving me the decency of a discussion, you *ran*."

"I will not be hidden away. Not again. I will not be your dirty secret. You will not drag me back to—" And then it was as if what he'd said caught up with her. She stopped short. Her breath came out in a loud, sharp gust. "What did you say?"

She looked so beautiful. So shocked by words he thought obvious. He thought it had been…a neon sign on his very face. That soft spot. That distraction his mother had accused him of.

And she seemed utterly and thoroughly shocked as if it had not occurred to her.

Because, clearly, it hadn't. A mix of his own failures, and perhaps some of her own.

But that also gave him hope now, instead of fury. Something to hold on to that might…lead them to where they needed to be.

He moved to her, and when she didn't back away, just stood there still staring at him as if he'd grown another head, he took her hands in his. He looked her in the eye. And he said the words this time—not yelling, not accusing, but with everything he felt inside of him.

"I love you, Beaugonia. My entire life I have been a tool. A payment to a debt. No one has ever cared what I might like or want. Not until *you*. You read what I asked you to. You enjoyed the chalet even though you hated the drive. You were honest with me—I *thought* you were honest with me. And then I discovered you had been hiding this…" He didn't have the word for it.

"Failure? Blight? Weakness?"

He stared at her. At the anger on her face. She didn't believe those things. Surely… Surely, she didn't believe those things. His self-possessed princess. And then it dawned on him.

When she had looked at him as though she didn't understand a word he was saying back at the chalet, he had been talking about his grandmother's words. The things she had passed down to him, whether he'd really considered the truth of them or not.

So these words were not *Beau's*. They were not even his. They had come before. They were her baggage. They were, no doubt, her father's words. And she didn't even realize it.

But they had likely been the words her father had used when he'd kept her hidden away, and it hadn't been all that long ago when he had threatened the very same. Maybe for different reasons, but that was the problem. They both had a lot of reasons they did not fully understand, they had not fully dealt with.

But now they would.

Beau was certain she was shaking, but Lyon's hands still held hers. He was looking at her like she'd suddenly started speaking in tongues.

"I have never once used those words to describe you, Beau," he said, very calmly. Very carefully. "I understand now why you thought I might, but I do not care about panic attacks. I have been on anxiety medication since I was fifteen. The state of your brain chemistry is not what dismayed me. It was that you lied and *hid* yourself from me."

She thought she had been floored when he claimed to love her, but this… He said it as if it was fine. As if… all his talk about stability and respectability had nothing to do with… He said he'd been on anxiety medication as if it was *nothing*.

"You've been on *what*?"

"I would not call what I had panic attacks, but the consistent cycle of catastrophic thinking was interfering with my studies. My mother…" He frowned a little as if he was realizing something. "Looking back, I think she was afraid if she did not do something, my grandmother would be…very unhappy with me. So she found me a therapist. I was prescribed medication. It has helped, infinitely."

"Helped," she echoed. Stupidly. But… It had never occurred to her in a million years that he might have anxieties. Real ones, not just his obsessive worry about respectability. An actual condition that needed some kind of interference. "I need to sit."

And he didn't let her go. He just led her to the couch and sat next to her when she all but collapsed into the seat.

"Beau, I do not think your panic attacks are any of those words you said. Those are *your* words. Not mine."

But as she sat there with the reality of all this…new information, she knew that wasn't exactly true. Not her own words. Not really. "I never cared about my panic attacks. Not in that…way. I can't help it, so I wasn't about to beat myself up about it."

"But your father did it for you."

She looked up into his eyes. Even before she'd loved him, she had always thought they were more alike than different, but this was… How could it be true that he understood so well? That they were *this much* alike?

I love you.

He had said that. Plainly and simply. In the midst of a very loud scene. Where he had yelled and not cared who heard.

"You really love me?" she asked on a whisper. "Even with…"

"I am here, *tesoruccia*. I told Mother to handle the dinner. I do not intend to make it back in time. I intend to make everything right. So that we can build a life together. One of balance and stability…but not…sacrificing ourselves on the altar of our images. Our people should know that *we* are people. Love. Soft spots. Anxieties."

It sounded too good to be true. And yet...

She thought of what Zia had said. About give-and-take. She had given, and she had taken—when he'd offered comfort, when he'd been kind. But only rarely had they *discussed what* they were doing, and so perhaps they hadn't had a chance to understand one another. Their gives and takes were careful, shrouded, because they had both been burned by people who should have loved them, but had only taken instead.

So much of him she understood—what had shaped him, why he felt the way he did even if she didn't agree, but she could admit now that she was perhaps not the best judge of understanding him when it came to *her*.

Because she had her own baggage clouding her judgment. But he was helping her see past that. Love had done that.

And when his baggage had clouded his judgment, he had used his words. He had told her about his legacy. About what he felt he had to do to pay that debt he thought he owed. Maybe he'd been wrong, but he'd never run away. He had been honest.

She had not been.

"I am sorry."

"You are?"

"I...jumped to conclusions. Based on my own issues. I was so...unhappy. But you said I made you happy and I wanted to. I wanted to do anything I could to make you happy. Because I love you, Lyon. Your kindness. That desire within you to do what is right. But I cannot be that thing you need. I cannot pretend as well as I wanted to. I don't wish to…sleep in the same bed every night so far apart. I don't think I am capable of being the robot you wanted. I—"

He squeezed her hands together. "It was wrong. Or at least, misguided. But we are learning. We will forge a new path. It will be…a challenge. We have the country's baggage stacked against us, but if we have learned to carry our own, if we help each other unpack our own, perhaps we can do the same as royals."

It sounded like a dream, but also…possible. And she wondered why it hadn't occurred to her. Why her own response to everything was all or nothing. Misery or run away. "I suppose we both need to work on our compromising."

His mouth curved, and she started to allow herself to hope…to really hope.

"I am quite sure my mother will come around eventually, but it will take time. Parliament might not care for it or me, but the citizens of Divio will. I believe they will. I cannot be perfect for them, or for you, though I will still try. But what I know I can be is there. I can find balance. If you'll share a life with me, Beau. I think we can accomplish anything."

Anything.

It was such a big promise, such a hopeful future. It made her realize how small her dreams had always been. Because she had never dreamed of a love that might not be concerned with her panic. She had not allowed herself to dream of…*anything* except the bare minimum.

"When I was a very little girl, the only thing I ever dreamed about was my own little place. Hidden away from my father. Just me and Zia. Lots of animals, but never people. I never truly believed anyone but Zia could see me for who I was."

He touched her cheek. *"Tesoruccia..."*

"You made an effort. To know me, to love me. You call me a treasure, and I have never felt like one until you. I'm sorry I didn't know how to make an effort back, to...believe you'd see something lovable. But I will learn. I promise to learn how to stay instead of run, to reach out instead of hide."

"Come home with me. Be my wife. My princess. Let us figure it all out, always together."

She pulled her hands from his, but only so she could wrap them around his neck. And he held on, even as her tears spilled over. He whispered endearments, words of love, rubbed her back. He gave her so much she'd never had, because though Zia had tried to be there for her, so much of their relationship was Zia acting as barrier between Father and her, not actually being able to *comfort.*

And it was scary, really, to believe that she might have something so beautiful, so wonderful, when she had spent so much of her life being told she wasn't good enough for it. When she hadn't realized how deep those scars went.

Until someone new had tried to love her. And it hadn't always been right or good. Because they were both flawed, in their own ways. But there was nothing inherently *wrong* with that. Not if you tried, not if you talked, not if you loved.

"You must only promise to never run away again," he murmured against her hair.

She nodded, still holding on to him. "I do. I promise. To work everything out, no matter how ridiculous either of us are being. I will not run away again, but you must promise the same."

He pulled away slightly, frowning down at her. "I never ran away."

"You did. You pulled away from me, hid yourself away from me. Perhaps it is not exactly the same, but it felt the same. Like a limb had been lost."

He nodded slowly. "Yes, exactly that. Then I promise, *amore mio*. With all that I am. I love you, Beau. I will always find a way to come back to that."

Beautiful words, but they were beautiful because he meant them. She could see it in his eyes, and because she knew him.

Lyon Traverso did not make promises he did not keep.

And this promise would last them a lifetime.

EPILOGUE

NINE CHILDREN WERE currently rolling in the snow outside the chalet high in the mountains of Divio. Muffled shrieks and laughter made their way into the kitchen where Beau stood hip to hip with her sister making a stew that would feed both their families tonight as they watched the goings-on from the large window.

It was moments like these, perfect, beautiful, crystallized togetherness—with the kids just far enough away not to be demanding all her attention—that Beau could feel completely full up with love and joy and relief that this was the life she got to lead.

Cristhian and Lyon were outside, dutifully pulling the younger children in sleds, aiding in the construction of snowmen, and breaking up fights that looked as if they'd turn physical in equal measure.

Five of the children outside were Zia's, and she would introduce a sixth in the coming months. Beau thought of her own pregnancy. Still new enough only Lyon knew so far, but they'd had a doctor's appointment before they'd herded the children up to the chalet for the holiday. All was well, and Beau wanted to tell her sister.

But for a moment, she just watched her husband and

her children. Her brother-in-law and her nieces and nephews. And allowed herself to be filled with gratitude.

Things had not always been smooth sailing, even after she'd gone back to Divio with Lyon. They had endured some growing pains as a newly married couple, and balance had been a slow, laborious process for them both to get comfortable with. There had been some difficulty getting pregnant with their first child. But then Lucia had come into the world, perfect and vibrant—with Beau's hazel eyes and Lyon's serious mouth.

She hadn't fixed everything, but the first grandchild Lyon had given his mother had certainly eased some of the bitterness between Beau and the countess.

With more children came more struggles, but more love. More hope. More joy. As a family, they had grown and evolved and *loved*. As a country, Divio had learned it could lean on Lyon as a leader. Also not smooth sailing. As Lyon had attempted to open up his country to more modern ways of thinking, allowing their eldest to be their heir despite being a girl, opening avenues of discussion about the importance of mental health, there had been stiff opposition. Much mudslinging. But Lyon had remained firm and fair, and the excellent leader he was. And he had been right, if they worked together, they could accomplish anything.

Since more citizens than not wanted these changes, parliament was hard-pressed to completely ignore the will of the people.

So Beau and Lyon had remained the crown prince and princess, popular with many. Particularly as their family grew.

"Do you ever sit back and pat yourself on the back?"

Zia asked her. They had finished the stew preparations, but still stood watching their families play.

"For what? Still having my hearing?"

Zia laughed. But she turned to Beau. "This all began with you. You helped me escape the castle for my weekend of freedom before I was supposed to settle down and marry Lyon. If you hadn't done that, I never would have met Cristhian."

"But if it wasn't for you running away, I never would have met or married Lyon."

"Technically, that was Father's doing."

"And Father is the one who hired Cristhian to find you. I guess we should be patting him on the back."

They shared and a look and then laughed.

"Never," Zia said firmly.

"Then I suppose we shall have to pat ourselves on the back for being brave enough to search for much better than he wanted for us."

"I like that," Zia said with a nod of her head. She looked outside once more, then gave Beau a sideways look. She leaned in close. "Are you pregnant?"

Beau scowled. "You never let me tell you!"

Zia shrieked and clapped her hands together, engulfing Beau in a hug. "Oh, they'll be so close together." Though age hadn't really mattered when it came to the Traverso and Sterling cousins. The pack were as close as siblings, begging to see more of each other all the time so that Zia and Cristhian had agreed to spend a good deal of their time in Divio these past few years.

Still, it was nice. To be in the same place, to share their experiences. No longer protectors or martyrs to each other. Just sisters. Living a wonderful life.

Zia pulled back, studied Beau's face. "My brood is still going to outnumber yours."

Which made Beau grin. Because that wasn't true at all. "Try again. I'm having twins this time. We'll be tied."

Zia laughed, then squeezed her tight again.

They had loved and protected each other first, and now they got to share in the love they'd learned how to share with their husbands, their children.

And when a pile of snow-covered children came rushing in, demanding warmth and food, followed by two snow-covered truly *good* men, Beau knew that all the romance books she'd always and still loved to read were right.

Love was everything.

* * * * *

Did Princess Bride Swap
leave you wanting more?

*Then you're bound to love the first installment in
the Rebel Princesses duet*
His Hidden Royal Heirs
*And why not dive into these other
Lorraine Hall stories?*

A Son Hidden from the Sicilian
The Forbidden Princess He Craves
Playing the Sicilian's Game of Revenge
A Diamond for His Defiant Cinderella
Italian's Stolen Wife

Available now!